# EROTICA SHORT STORIES, VOL. 10

I0683876

## Just Plain Bob

# Stuffed
# HARD

## WITH 6 FORBIDDEN STORIES

# WARNING

This book contains sexually explicit scenes and adult language. It may be considered offensive to some readers. This book is for sale to adults ONLY.

\* \* \* \* \* \* \* \* \* \* \* \* \* \* \* \* \* \* \*

Please store your files wisely where they cannot be accessed by underage readers.

Please feel free to send me an email. Just know that these emails are filtered by my publisher. Good news is always welcome.

Just Plain Bob - **justplainbob@awesomeauthors.org**

### About the Publisher

**4Fun Publishing**, a member of **BLVNP Incorporated**, 340 S. Lemon #6200, Walnut CA 91789, info@blvnp.com / legal@blvnp.com
NOTE: Due to the highly emotional reaction of some people to works of erotic fiction, any email sent to the above address that contains foul language or religious references is automatically deleted by our anti-spam software and will not be seen. All other communications are welcome.

### DISCLAIMER

Please don't be stupid and kill yourself. This book is a work of FICTION. Do not try any new sexual practice that you find in this book. It is fiction and not to be confused with reality. Neither the author nor the publisher or its associates assume any responsibility for any loss, injury, death or legal consequences resulting from acting on the contents in this book. Every character in this book is over 18 years of age. The author's opinions are not to be construed as the opinions of the publisher. The material in this book is for entertainment purposes ONLY. Enjoy.

Erotica Short Stories, Vol. 10

# Stuffed Hard

## With 6 Forbidden Stories

By: Just Plain Bob

© **Just Plain Bob 2015**
ISBN: 978-1-68030-278-3

The Writer

The Purse

The Project

The Phony Excuse

The Personal Assistant

The Truth About Maggie

# The Writer

I got up from the computer with a smile on my face. If I was right, within the next twenty-four hours, my husband would read what I had just typed and if I knew him—and believe me I did—he would be smiling and rubbing his cock. Hell, he might even take it out and stroke it.

Revenge could sometimes be so sweet!

\*\*\*

It all started the day I overheard two women gossiping at the beauty parlor. My favorite stylist had quit working at my regular salon and had gone to work at another place so I followed her. I'd only been coming to the place for three weeks so I didn't know them, and they had no idea who I was.

"Have you heard about Sophie?"

"Lord, what has that girl been up to now?"

"She's playing around with a married man again."

"Oh my. You would think that she would have learned by now. What's this one, her third?"

"Fourth, that's what I know."

"There was George Wilson and Bill Hallman that I knew about. Who was the third?"

"Dave Misner."

"Oh no. I thought Dave and Cheri were the perfect couple. No way would I have ever thought Dave would run around on Cheri."

"The story I got is that Cheri was having an affair with her fitness instructor and Dave found out. He took up with Sophie to rub Cheri's nose on it."

"What happened? I saw Dave and Cheri at church last Sunday."

"I guess they decided that they were even and that they still love each other. They are trying to put things back together. I think Sophie thought Dave was going to leave Cheri for her."

"That's what she thought about George Wilson and Bill Hillman. You would think by now that the girl would have a clue. Who is the latest one?"

"I don't know his name, but he is the tall, dark-haired man who runs the feed store."

That got my attention! My husband Steve is tall and dark haired, and he ran a feed store. In fact, it was the only feed store in town. Until hearing those two gossiping, I had never, not in ten years of marriage, ever considered that my husband was anything other than one-hundred percent faithful.

The two women changed the subject and moved on to something else, and I sat there and tried to think of something—anything at all—that I could look at and say that it was a sign of cheating but I couldn't. Steve could not have possibly been cheating on me. Unfounded rumors and gossip is all that it was.

On the way home from the beauty parlor, I tried to think about when Steve could cheat on me if he was, and I was pretty sure that I could account for all of his time. There were only three times during the week that he wasn't with me, and I knew where he was during those times. He bowled in a men's house league on Mondays and Thursdays and he had a lodge meeting on Wednesdays. I was not home alone on those nights. Monday I taught a class in pottery making at the community college and Thursday nights were my bridge-club nights. Wednesday was my quiet time. No, I could account for all of Steve's time so he couldn't be running around on me.

But still?

The seed had been planted and for two weeks it grew until it finally reached a point where I had to know for sure. I called my friend, Wanda, and told her I was going to have to miss the bridge night on Thursday and then I called the school and told them I had an out-of-town emergency and wouldn't be in on Monday.

On Monday, I parked down the street from the feed store when it closed. I followed Steve to the bowling alley, and just about the time I started feeling stupid for doubting him I noticed something odd. He didn't get out of his car. He just sat there, and I noticed him checking his watch every couple of minutes. Maybe ten minutes went by, and then another car pulled in and parked next to him, and a blond with big tits got out of that car and got in the car with Steve. They leaned together and kissed, and then Steve pulled out of the bowling alley parking lot. I followed them to Motel 6 and watched as Steve went into the office and got a room.

I sat where I could watch the door of room 119. It was three hours before Steve and his slut came out. They drove back to the bowling alley, made out for a few minutes, and then the fuck pig got out of Steve's car and got in her own as Steve pulled out of the lot and headed home.

Steve was waiting for me when I got home. He was smiling and he said, "I'm in the mood, sweetie. How about you?"

I wanted to pick up the table lamp and smack him with it, but instead I did something I had never done in out ten years of marriage. I told him that I had a splitting headache and didn't feel like it. He was shocked! I almost laughed, but that would not have fit the mood I was trying to project.

"In fact, honey, I feel so bad that I'm going to sleep in the spare bedroom tonight. I may even call in sick to work if I don't feel better in the morning."

That really got his attention. In nine years, I had never missed a scheduled day of work so I must really be sick. And it was true. I was sick—sick of looking at his sorry ass so I went off to bed. I avoided Steve on Tuesday morning, and I was in bed faking being sick when he got home from work. On Wednesday, I parked where I parked on Monday. When Steve got off work he went straight to the Motel 6 and got a room. He parked in front of room 107 and left the door open when he went inside. Ten minutes later the bimbo showed up, looked in the open door, saw Steve, and went inside and closed the door.

I sat there staring at that door and wondered what Steve saw in the cunt. I was better looking than she was. The only thing she had me beat on was her breast size. I was a 34B cup and she was at least a 38D. Steve had never indicated to me that he was a breast man. The one time I did mention getting a boob job he came unglued and told me that mine were perfect and not to touch them. What else did the cunt have going for her besides tits? I treated Steve like a fucking king for Christ's sake and he was out screwing around on me? I didn't wait to see what time Steve and his cunt would come out of the room. I just went home and was in bed pretending to be asleep when Steve got there.

I could have passed on Thursday, but I had already told the girls that I wouldn't be there and I guess I did have some morbid curiosity so I was again parked down the street when Steve closed the store. I followed him to an apartment complex on Wilcox and watched as he went up to an apartment and rang the bell. The door opened and the fucking big titted slut stepped aside and let Steve in. I wondered why Steve was wasting money on a motel room when the whore had an apartment. I also started wondering how long Steve had been fucking around on me. He had been going bowling for the last seven years and he had been a member of the lodge for nine. Had he been cheating on me that long?

I sat there in the apartment complex parking lot and tried to understand what was happening. Up until that day at the beauty parlor, I thought I had a great marriage and a loving husband. What had I done wrong?

I know that it wasn't the lack of sex. I had never, at least not until the last few days, said no when Steve wanted to make love. We averaged five times a week and I've been told that after ten years of marriage that level of frequency is almost unbelievable and I did everything for Steve, including oral and anal. It made no sense to me. I knew that I was better looking than Steve's slut. Hell, I had guys hitting on me all the time, but I had never been unfaithful to my husband. At least not until then. I started to give some serious thought to getting even by doing the same thing that Steve was doing.

As I pulled up in front of the house I saw flickering light through the front window and was confused for a second before I realized that Steve must have left the computer on again. Once inside I saw the screen saver scrolling across the screen and out of curiosity, I hit the Enter key to clear out the screen saver and show me what Steve was logged on to when he left. It was another one of his porn sites and what was on the screen was a story of some kind. I read some of it and found that it was a story about a cheating wife. I hit the Back key and found another story about a cheating wife. I hit Back again and then again and again. All stories about wives cheating on their husbands: some, because they liked bigger cocks; some, because they just were not being taken care of at home; some, because they had gotten drunk and were taken advantage of and found out that it was exciting and a turn on to cheat; and some, because they were being blackmailed for something or other. I pulled up History and found that Steve had four story sites that he visited regularly. Was that it? Was Steve cheating for the thrill and excitement of it? I shut the computer down and went to take a shower.

I was washing my hair when the idea came to me. I rolled it around in my mind and by the time I was toweling off I knew just how I was going to get back at Steve. The first thing I would have to do was get back into the loving wife mode, get back to not saying no when Steve wanted to make love (No, better change that to fuck. There would be no precious little love making in that house anymore). I would even go after him. He had to think that it was business as usual. There would be no confrontation over Miss Big Tits. Steve would never find out that I knew. That was important to me—that he doesn't find out that I knew because my revenge was going to be ongoing. If our marriage lasted fifty years, it would be fifty years of hanging horns on him and then letting him read about it. Every affair, every back seat quickie, every surreptitious blow job in the supply closet at work would be written up in story form and then posted to the sites that Steve accessed and he would read them and not know that he was the cuckold in the story. And I knew just who the first one to cuckold my hubby would be.

Our next door neighbor Jason is a hunk and he has made no secret of the fact that he would fuck me in a New York minute if I would let him. Never in front of Steve of course and even with me he couches it in terms that will allow him to protest his innocence if I call him on it. I will admit that I do flirt with him at times, sometimes outrageous, but up until Miss Big Tits came on the scene, Jason didn't have a chance in hell of ever getting a sniff of my pussy. But the big-titted whore was on the scene and Jason was finally going to get lucky.

*** 

The first thing I did was rent a post office box. The second was to buy a laptop computer and the third was to sign up with an ISP using the post office box as the billing address. I bought the laptop to ensure that Steve would never know I was writing stories. If I used our home computer, there was always a chance he could stumble onto something. I wouldn't even let him know I had a laptop.

Using my new laptop I accessed the four sites that Steve spent his time on. It was a simple matter to set up an author's account on each of the four sites. I had to select a user name and a password and I was in business. I thought long and hard about what user name to select and finally went with "pissedoffwife." In the author's profile on each site, I let everyone know that I was a wife who had been cheated on and that I had set out to get even and that all the stories I posted would be true. Once I had all that in place I set out to get Jason's cock in me.

***

I was paid for teaching my class on Monday nights so that night was out, but I could take time off from my bridge club. They had a list of people who liked filling in so I wouldn't be putting them behind the eight ball. I worked a lot of extra hours at work and I built up those extra hours as comp time and I had quite a bit I could use when I wanted. And I had my "quiet time" Wednesday nights plus Steve played golf on weekends that he didn't work and he sometimes took off on weekend hunting and fishing trips. I would have plenty of time to "play."

I would make my move on Jason Saturday morning. Steve would be playing golf and the weather was supposed to be sunny and hot; perfect conditions for what I wanted to make happen.

I was awake when Steve got home from his meeting with his fuck pig. I was lying on the bed wearing a black lace nightie and my legs were spread wide as I worked on my pussy with a rubber cock that we sometimes used for sex play. When Steve came into the room, I smiled at him and said:

"I'm feeling much better, sugar bear and I'm glad you are home. I hope I won't be needing this anymore." and I tossed the rubber cock aside. "Come on, baby, show Miss Kitty how much you missed her."

Steve smiled and stripped off his clothes while I watched him and mentally prepared myself for what was going to be the most distasteful part of the charade. We almost always started our love making sessions with oral sex and I was dreading having to suck Steve's cock while he still had the juices of his fuck pig on it, but it would have to be done if I were to convince him that things were normal.

Steve surprised me. He bypassed all foreplay and moved between my spread legs and I had to wonder if it was because he didn't feel right having me suck his cock so soon after soaking it in another woman's cunt or was he afraid I might taste her and then ask him what he had been up to.

The rubber cock had gotten me wet and I'd helped out some by using some KY lotion (I wanted Steve to get used to a "wet" me) so Steve slid right in. I clamped my legs on his waist, dug my nails into his ass, and told him to fuck me.

"I need it, baby, do me fast and hard. Make me cum, lover, make me cum."

He did make me cum, and then he came, pulled out, rolled over and in minutes he was asleep. I looked at him lying there and lightly snoring and sarcastically thought, "Poor tired, baby. It must be exhausting having to fuck two different women in the space of four hours." And then of course I wondered how many times he had gotten it up for his slut pig and then I thought of something else that hadn't yet occurred to me. Did he eat the bitch? On Mondays, Wednesdays, and Thursdays I was going to have to fight hard not to barf when Steve kissed me.

On Friday night, Steve was horny and we fucked twice. I did suck his cock, but it didn't upset me because he had showered that morning so whatever remained of his whore was washed off. Before we went to sleep, he reminded me that he would be playing golf in the morning and then covering the feed store from noon to closing. I smiled as I thought, "Okay, asshole, you go play with your little white ball and if I work it right, I'll have some balls to play with too."

\*\*\*

Steve was up and out the door at 6:45 AM on Saturday, and I lounged in bed for another two hours and then I got up, had coffee, and dug out what I was going to wear. I put on a pair of "Daisy Dukes" (with no panties) and a tank top. I didn't bother to wear a bra under. Once dressed, if you could call it that, I went outside and started weeding the flower beds on the south side of the house, (Jason was my neighbor to the south) knowing that sooner or later Jason would notice me.

Bending over pulling weeds put my ass cheeks on full display, and it wasn't ten minutes before I heard Jason say:

"Does Steve know that you are out here teasing me?"

"Teasing you? How in the world do you figure that? All I'm doing is pulling weeds out of my flower beds."

"You might as well be naked from the waist down. Those shorts don't cover anything. At least they aren't covering the good parts."

"I always thought you were interested in my good parts."

"I am. I just wish that I could see more."

"How much more?"

"It would be nice if I could see all of it."

"Oh, I'll just bet it would be. But it would be very irresponsible of me to let you see all of it."

"How so?"

"Can you not just imagine the state that it would leave you? Would you want me to walk around all day carrying the guilt and all that discomfort you would give me?"

"You could avoid the guilt by taking care of the problem."

"I suppose that would work, but somehow I don't think that Steve would care for that."

"Fuck Steve!"

"Fuck Steve? I thought it was me that you wanted."

"I do want you, sexy little bitch. It is all I can do to keep from jumping this fence."

I pulled my tank top off and dropped it on the ground. I stood there and caressed my breasts with my hands and said:

"Is this enough to make you want to jump the fence?"

He just stood there staring at me with open mouth. I pushed the Dukes down and kicked them away. I gave him a good look at my clean shaven beaver.

"How about this? Fence jumping material? The front door is unlocked," I said as I turned and walked into the house.

The stairway to the upstairs is just inside the front door and I was sitting on the second step, legs spread wide, and fingering my pussy when the front door opened and Jason came in. "What took you so long?" I asked as I watched Jason hurriedly strip. He walked toward me with his hard cock leading the way, and I had to move up one step so my mouth would be on the same level as his erection. I opened my mouth and he walked his cock right into it. As my lips clamped around the first cock other than my husband's to see the inside of my mouth, I smiled as I thought of Steve reading about it.

I sucked Jason's hard cock until I got him to cum. I swallowed all of it and then stood up. "I have until five this afternoon to play. Are you up for it?"

"I'm sure that you will be able to take care of the 'up' part."

"Oh, you can be sure of that, honey. Come on. Let's take this to the bedroom."

Once there, Jason pushed me down on my back and said, "My turn," as he pushed my legs apart and went down on me. The man knew how to eat pussy. I let him munch on me until he had me close to the edge and I needed a hard cock so I pushed him away, moved over on top of him and guided his cock up into me as I pushed down on him. I moved up and down on his hard cock and moaned:

"Come on honey, fuck me. Make me your slut."

"I've always wanted my very own slut," he said as he worked his hard rod into me.

"Do it right, honey, and I'll be your slut whenever you want."

"Ah, incentive. Incentive is good."

I bounced and rocked on him until he finally moaned and rolled me over on my back and fucked me hard and fast. He got me off twice before he had his own climax and then he pulled out and settled down on the bed next to me.

"Was I good enough? Did I do it right? Are you going to be my slut now?" he said as he faked panting like a dog expecting a reward.

"You did just fine, honey. Consider me your fuck-toy from now on. Just one major problem."

"What's that?"

"You are soft and we still have hours before Steve will be home."

"I'm betting that my little fuck-toy can cure that soft condition. Come on, sweet slut, put it in your mouth."

We sucked and fucked off and on for the rest of the afternoon and before Jason left, I told him I would sneak over to his place for a quickie the next day and I did—twice! Once in the morning and once in the afternoon.

I was waiting on the stairs for Steve when he got home that night. I was exactly the same as I was for Jason when he had walked through that door, and I did exactly the same thing to Steve what I had done for Jason, and then I led him up to the bedroom for his 'seconds'. They weren't sloppy seconds—I had cleaned myself out—since I didn't want to give Steve any idea that he wasn't the first one in me that day, but I did want to give him my pussy that had been well used by someone else. As I lay there looking at him as he thrust into me, I thought, "That's it, asshole, fuck this pussy. This pussy isn't yours any more. It belongs to Jason now, Jason and what I hope will be a whole lot of others, and you just get to use it from time to time after someone else has used it."

*** 

I finished typing the story of my afternoon with Jason in the laptop, making only minor changes to disguise Jason, Steve, and me. Things like changing Jason's name to Jonas, changing feed store to gas station and making Jason my north side neighbor instead of my south side one. And of course, I changed Steve's name and mine. I added the disclaimer that the names had been changed to protect the guilty, and then I sent the story off to the four sites. Hopefully, if my wish was granted, Steve would be sitting at the computer stroking his cock as he would read the story and think that some guys had all the luck.

I got up and started the laundry. As I was separating the whites from the coloreds I was thinking of who else I could be a slut for. I was going to need lots of material for my husband to beat off to.

**End of the 1<sup>st</sup> Story**

# The Purse

I knew the fridge was empty, so I made a shopping list during my afternoon break. On the way home from work, I stopped by Safeway. I grabbed a cart, hit the courtesy counter to get my lottery tickets for that night's drawing, and then headed for the produce section.

I am not a picky shopper. I know what I'm after so I pretty much grab and go. I'm not one to pick up a head of lettuce or a green pepper and roll it around in my hands in minutes, inspecting it before dropping it in my cart. The exception, of course, is eggs. I always—always—open the carton and make sure that none of them are broken.

I'd picked up the makings for a salad and was pushing my cart toward the fruit when I saw her. She was standing next to the tomatoes and she had one in her hand and was checking it out like her life depended on it being absolutely flaw free. She was pretty, not a raving beauty but not bad to look at from the waist up. But from the waist down? Oh my fucking God! I was instantly in heat.

My major turn on have always been legs, nylons, and high heels. She was fairly tall, maybe five eight, and it looked like four feet of that was leg. She had a skirt on that fell to just below the knee and she was wearing hose and heels, and not just any old heels but the super sexy heels that don't seem to be much more than a collection of very thin leather straps attached to a sole and supported by a four-inch heel. It was the kind of shoe worn by a woman who knew she had great legs and wanted to show them off.

My plan to get in, get what I needed, and get out suddenly changed. I rarely got to see what this girl was showing, and I decided that I was going to take my time shopping and do it not too far away from where she was doing hers. For the next twenty-five minutes, I was never more than ten feet away from her as we wandered up and down the aisles. I ended up with far more in my cart that I had planned on getting, but I had to at least make the pretense of shopping as I followed her around and feasted on the visual treat she presented.

When it was time to head for the checkout stands she got in a faster one than I did and I saw her walk out of the store as my checker took her time in ringing me up. I figured that I had seen the last of my leggy beauty. I had never seen her around before, so the odds were that I wouldn't likely see her again.

I finally cleared the checkout stand and pushed my cart out of the store and toward my car, and I saw her again. She was parked about six cars beyond mine and she was unloading her cart into the trunk of her car. She was putting the last bag into the trunk as I started down the parking aisle toward her. She walked away from her cart, got in the car, and drove off. I saw that she had left her purse in the small fold-down tray that is in the shopping cart, and I hollered at her and waved my arms to try and stop her, but she kept on going.

I decided got her purse from her cart, loaded my groceries into my car, went back into the store, and turn the purse in at the courtesy counter. But first, I decided to look in the purse and check out the girl's driver's license to see if she lived close enough to me that I could contrive some way to see more of her. Just as soon as I had that thought, it occurred to me that I had the means to see more of her right in my hands. To hell with taking it to the counter, I'd deliver it to her.

\*\*\*

I knocked on the door to apartment 3A and waited. I figured that she was home because I saw the car where she loaded her groceries in the parking lot. It never occurred to me until after I'd knocked that the girl might not be single. Maybe some humongous hairy dude would answer the door. I guess it didn't matter since I could hand the purse to him just as easily as I could hand it to her, but a big hairy dude was not what I had hoped to see as I drove over.

I saw the light coming through the security peephole go away so I knew someone was on the other side of the door. I heard the security chain rattle—putting it on or taking it off, I wondered—and then the door opened about six inches, and I saw that it was the former. The girl looked through the gap at me and said:

"You're the creep who followed me through the store."

"Yeah, that was me."

"You better get out of here before I call the cops and turn you in for stalking me."

"I don't think that you want to do that. They might ask me why I'm here and that could be bad for you."

"Bad for me?"

"Yeah, honey, very, very bad for you. They would ask me why I was here," and I lifted up her purse and showed it to her, "and I would tell them that you left your purse in your shopping cart and I brought it here to you. Then one of them, they travel in pairs you know, would say, 'Is that her purse?' and I would say yes and he would put out his hand for it so he could open it, look inside for your license to verify my story and that it was indeed your purse. He would be looking for your driver's license, but he would find the same thing I did when I looked. Now I have no experience in these things so I'm willing to believe that the little cellophane bags full of white stuff are powdered sugar that you carry with you because you don't like to put granular sugar in your coffee or tea but the fuzz may not be so trusting. That is also the reason that I didn't turn the purse in at the store. They more than likely would have looked for your license to call you and tell you they had your purse, but they just might have called the cops.

"I'm a leg lover, honey, and looking at your gorgeous pins as you walked around the store made my day and for that reason alone, I don't want to see you headed for a jail cell."

I handed her the purse through the partially opened door and said, "Best be a little more careful with it, honey. The next guy that finds it might not be near as nice."

I turned and walked away without a backward glance. Fantastic legs and sexy high heels were not near enough to get me to spend time with someone who used what I found in her purse. No, thank you!

\*\*\*

Two months later, I was at a retirement party for Mark Whipple who had been my boss for the last seven years when I saw Adrianna again. I remembered her name from her driver's license, and I wondered who she had come to the party with. She obviously knew how great an asset her legs were because she was showing them off by wearing a short skirt and four-inch heels. She was talking to Mark when I walked into the room, and she saw me almost as soon as I saw her. She said something to Mark and he turned and looked at me and then went back to talking with her. I couldn't help but wonder what was up with that.

I walked over to the bar and ordered a vodka tonic and then set out to socialize and mingle. After I'd been there maybe twenty minutes, Mark came up to me and said:

"You need to watch yourself, Rob."

"Why is that, boss?"

"You have caught the attention of my niece, Adrianna. She asked me all about you. If she comes at you be careful."

"Why would she come at me?"

"No idea, but she did show an interest. Be careful, son, she can be pretty overwhelming at times."

I was thinking, "Don't I know it?" as he walked away and I remembered what I'd found in her purse. I spent another hour socializing and then I got my coat and got ready to leave. The coat-check girl was handing me my coat when I heard:

"You were really going to leave without saying hi to me?"

I turned and saw Adrianna standing there. "Why would I say hi to you? The last time I saw you, you called me a creep and threatened to call the cops on me. What was I supposed to do? Walk up to you and say 'Hi. Called the cops on anybody lately?' I don't think so."

"Oh come on. Cut me some slack here. Put yourself in my position. A man follows you around for almost half an hour in a store and then shows up at your apartment and knocks on your door. You would have had the same thoughts I did and don't forget that you didn't let me know that you were returning my purse until after you had me thinking that you were a stalker."

"Oh, yes, your purse. How could I forget your purse? Why would a one-hundred-percent straight arrow like myself want to speak to the kind of person who had what you had in your purse?"

"Maybe the person isn't the kind of person you think she is. Maybe you could buy this person a cup of coffee at the Denny's on the corner and give her a chance to tell you all about what you saw."

I looked at her for a couple of seconds and thought, "Why not? What could it hurt?" And so I told her that I would meet her at the Denny's in five minutes.

"I'll go with you. I came with my Uncle Mark and I've already told him that you will be giving me a ride home."

"That was taking a hell of a chance."

"I didn't think so. Any guy trying to keep me out of jail because he liked my legs would seem like a safe bet. Besides, you wouldn't want to disappoint my Uncle Mark, would you?"

On the ride to the restaurant I found out that she had lived with

Mark from the time she was twelve until she got married. He was her only living relative when her parents were killed in an accident and he took her in and raised her.

"You are married?"

"Divorced. You?"

"Was, but it was many long years ago."

"You over her? It took me a long time to get over him."

"If the attachment was that strong, why did it end?"

"He had forsaken all other issues."

"Forsaking all other issues?"

"In that, he didn't. When he didn't forsake my cousin Beth I ended it. How about you?"

"With mine it wasn't my cousin, but it was just as bad. He was my boss at that time. She told me that it meant nothing, that it was only just sex and she only did it to help me get me a promotion."

"Did you get the promotion?"

"My chances for advancement died when I broke his nose and three ribs and caused him to lose one of his testicles."

"And you didn't go to jail?"

"He wouldn't press charges after I told him I would sue him for alienation of affections and a half-dozen other sexual charges. Did you know that you can sue for sexual harassment if your boss goes after your spouse, promising to help you in your career?"

"Why didn't you sue? Wouldn't it have been just as satisfying to ruin him financially as it was hurting him?"

"According to the attorney I had at the time, my wife, since we were still married, would have gotten half of it in the divorce settlement and no way was I going to let that bitch profit from cheating on me."

In the booth at Denny's I got the story about the cellophane packets that I had found in her purse.

"They weren't mine. I was at a club with my girlfriend Gloria and the guy she was dating at the time. I was out on the dance floor so I didn't see it, but apparently Gary, the guy she was dating, saw a couple of guys come in that he knew were on the narcotics squad. The problem was that they also knew him. Before they saw him, he gave Gloria what he was carrying and she put it in her purse, grabbed mine, came out onto the dance floor, and told me that she needed to talk to me urgently. We went to the ladies room and she asked me to take the stuff and then she and Gary would leave and draw the cops off, and while they were busy either following or searching Gary, I could slip out the back door and meet them later and give the stuff back to them.

"I hadn't gone back to the table so the cops wouldn't associate me with Gary. She left the bathroom and I was supposed to wait five minutes or so and then go and sit at the bar until I saw her leave with Gary, but after she left, I started thinking about how stupid it would be to sit around with a bunch of drugs with known narcotics officers in the building. I hid the stuff and then went home. I went back to the club the next day when the cops were gone and picked the stuff up. I stopped by Safeway and went home. When you came to the door, I thought it was Gloria until I looked through the peep hole and saw you. I do not use that stuff, never have, and never will."

"And it is important that I know this why?"

"Uncle Mark speaks highly of you so you can't be all bad. You seem to really like my legs and you did try to keep me out of jail. A guy with all of those qualities just might be a good guy to know."

"Can this be considered as you making a move on me?"

"See? Another good quality. You are bright and perceptive. What do you think? Want to give it a try?"

"I can't remember the last time a girl came after me. In fact, I'm almost sure that it never happened. I just have to say okay if for no other reason than the sheer uniqueness of it. Then of course there are those sexy legs."

And that is how my relationship with Adrianna got started.

\*\*\*

I'd already been through a bad marriage and I was in no great hurry to do it again. Gail and I had married after knowing each other for only six months. I don't know if a longer relationship before proposing would have made any difference, but if I ever got married again, I was going to know my bride a whole lot better than I knew Gail when I said I do.

Adrianna and I started out dating a couple of times a week, and as we got to know each other better we saw each other more often. We kissed on our second date. I got my hands on her breasts on the fifth date, and my fingers inside her panties on our seventh. When I took her home after our eighth, she asked:

"How long are we going to dance around it? I'm past being ready for it."

I knew what she was asking and said, "I'm more than ready too, but I was letting you set the pace. I didn't want to push too hard and risk scaring you away."

She was magnificent in the bedroom. Enthusiastic, energetic, responsive, and she loved it all. I warmed her up with some pussy licking and clit sucking, and she pushed me into a sixty-nine. We made love missionary, she sucked me hard again, and she went cowgirl. And then she asked me to take her ass. The first time in my life that a girl wanted anal, the first time we fucked, and I had never—never—had a girl asked me for it.

We fell asleep cuddled up to each other, and in the morning she woke me up with a blow job and then climbed aboard and rode me cowgirl until we both got off. We showered together which ended up with us back on the bed which led to a second shower. She fixed breakfast for us and afterward she had me do her on the kitchen table. After that night, we never went out that we didn't end up in either her bed or mine.

Adrianna, or Ri as I called her, and I had an awful lot in common. We both liked to read, liked a full range of music from classical to bluegrass, liked hiking in the mountains, and loved country western dancing. The only thing I didn't like where Ri was concerned was that she had a few friends that I would just as soon she didn't have. Gloria was her best friend and the fact that Gloria hung with drug dealers, druggies and other losers didn't bother Ri at all, but other than finding reasons for not spending time around Gloria (had to work late, change the oil in my car, pick the lint out of my navel) I stayed away from the issue. After a few initial comments about it where I carefully mentioned that sooner or later, Gloria was going to be looking at some jail time when she ended up being with her drug-selling boyfriend when he got busted, I wisely kept my mouth shut about things. I knew how things would go if I tried to come between her and her best friend.

On her part, she absolutely detested my cousin Lou and didn't care if I knew it or not. I didn't much care because Lou was a bit obnoxious, but I was used to him. She did like my mom and dad and while they had been lukewarm where Gail was concerned, they thought that Ri was an absolute gem.

***

After six months of dating, Ri and I decided to move in together. She gave up her apartment and moved into the house that I had managed to hang onto when Gail and I went through our divorce. After four months of cohabitation, I decided that I would like to make things permanent and I proposed.

"Are you serious?"

"Sure. After ten months together, including four as pretend man and wife, why not?"

"I don't know. I never thought about it. Things were going so well. Marriage would change things."

"Like what?"

"I don't know. I just know that marriage changes things."

"Well, love, it is up to you. If you would rather keep things just as they are, we can."

"I'm happy with our relationship, honey. I'm just scared to do anything that might change it."

"Like I said, Ri, it is up to you. I love you, and I want to spend all my time with you with or without a ring on your finger."

"I love you too, honey. It doesn't have to be a big wedding, does it?"

"Not if you don't want one. Is that some kind of a yes?"

"I guess it is."

"Great. We can get the blood tests and license this week and I'll line up a justice of the peace for next week."

"No, not next week. Next week and the week after that, I'll be involved in a large project at work and I'll probably have to work late a couple of nights and maybe even a Saturday. Let me get that out of the way first."

Three weeks later we took our vows in front of my mom and dad, her Uncle Mark and her best friend Gloria and Gloria's current boyfriend. I say current because her drug-dealing boyfriend got busted and was in jail. Fortunately for Gloria, she wasn't with him at the time.

\*\*\*

The next five years flew by and my marriage with Ri was everything that I could have hoped for. Our friends all thought that we were the perfect couple and had the perfect marriage, and as far as I was concerned, they were right. Naturally, there were problems, but not very many, and most of them had to do with her job.

Twice her job had forced me to make some major changes in plans that I had made, and it was always for the same reason. She would get on a major project with an approaching deadline and she would end up working late and on weekends. The first time, I'd scored some tickets to a concert and surprised her with them only to get the bad news that she was going to be working late the week of the concert.

The second time really pissed me off. A friend had signed up for a ten-day cruise in the Caribbean and then there was a death in the family. He had paid in advance and the tickets were not refundable. I offered to buy them from him and be damned if Ri would have another project that she had to work.

But hey, they were just some minor glitches and nothing to really lose any sleep over.

\*\*\*

Everything was going great, and then I let a few beers too many make me stupid and I invited the serpent into the Garden of Eden.

One night, Ri was doing something with her Uncle Mark so I stopped after work to have a couple of beers and shoot some pool at my favorite sports bar. Jimmy and some guy I didn't know were on one of the tables when I got there. Jimmy was one of the few guys that Gloria had gone out with who I liked. I challenged the winner and when Jimmy won, we played. Jimmy was damned near unbeatable that night, and I lost. I got out of the way of the next challenger who also lost. The next challenger was the guy Jimmy had been playing when I got there. He lost and joined me at my table and we introduced ourselves. His name was Paul and he was a good friend of Jimmy. We talked about sports and drank beer as we kept challenging the table and losing.

Finally, a guy beat Jimmy and he joined us at the table. When Jimmy sat down, he looked from me to Paul and then back at me as he said:

"Weird that you two should find each other at the same table."

"Why is that?" I asked.

"You are married to Adrianna and Paul used to be."

"Used to be what?"

"Married to Adrianna."

I turned to Paul. "Is that true? Are you Ri's ex?"

"'fraid so. I heard that she married again. So you're the guy, huh?"

"Yep, and I want to thank you for it."

"Thank me? Why would you thank me?"

"If you hadn't screwed up, Ri would never have divorced you and I would never have met her."

"I screwed up? I don't know what kind of bullshit she fed you, but I didn't screw anything up and she didn't divorce me, I divorced her."

"She said that she caught you screwing her cousin."

"She doesn't have a cousin. Her only living relative is her Uncle Mark."

"She wouldn't lie to me. I can understand you not wanting to look bad, but I know her and she wouldn't lie to me."

"Have it your way. She wouldn't lie to you. I'm the bad guy. For all I know, she hasn't seen Daniel since our divorce."

"Daniel?"

"Never mind. You are happy with her so let it be."

Well of course I couldn't let it be. No way was I going to let the asshole cast aspersions on my wife so I said:

"No. Who is this Daniel and what does he have to do with this?"

He shrugged and said, "Okay. Daniel was her first love and for all I know he still is. They dated all through high school and he got her cherry and promised to marry her. Then his dad got a promotion that caused them to move out of state. She met me in our first year in college and we ended up getting married. Then Daniel came back to town, they hooked up, and she cheated on me. It happened three more times over the course of the next five years, only the third time, she was seen by my sister going into a motel with him. My sister told me and I confronted Adrianna. She admitted it, but said that it didn't mean anything. She really loved me, but she had a special attachment to Daniel. Besides, it was only every couple of years or so and none of the previous times had hurt us any.

"If I was a different kind of guy I might have bought into it and let him have her once every couple of years or so, but I'm not that kind of a guy. She was either mine totally or she wasn't mine at all. Since she wasn't mine totally, she was out."

"That just doesn't sound like Adrianna. It doesn't sound at all like something she would do."

"Maybe she learned her lesson with me or then again, maybe Daniel never came back to town."

"No, I'm sorry, but I can't believe you. That just isn't my Ri."

"Tell you what. Meet me here tomorrow and buy me a beer and I'll show you the divorce papers that say I divorced her cheating ass for infidelity."

He could see on my face that I thought he was a liar so he said, "Let me ask you something. It doesn't happen all that often, maybe once very couple of years, but does she suddenly get on special projects and have to work late and on the weekends? If she does, it means that Daniel is in town. If it hasn't happened, then one of the two things I mentioned has happened. She learned a lesson or Daniel has never come back to town."

I had a lot to think about as I drove home, and the thoughts I was having were not good ones. If I hadn't pushed I could have disregarded Paul's assertion that he wasn't at fault in the divorce, as male bluster being put in a bad light, but I had pushed and he had dropped "the working late on special projects" bomb on me, and then there was that one little item that I had never picked up on even though I should have. How could he have been caught fucking a cousin that she didn't have?

Now I had a head full of thoughts that I really didn't want to have. Chief among them was the fact that Adrianna had done the "special projects" thing to me three times over the past five years and the first time was just weeks before we married.

Ri and I averaged making love four times a week and we made love at the same frequency during the times she worked on her "special projects" which led to a disturbing thought. Was I getting sloppy seconds during those periods? I hadn't noticed any change in her behavior during those times. I didn't see any lessening of love or affection during those periods nor did I see any increase that might have indicated some sort of guilty feelings on her part.

Yes indeed, I did have a lot of thoughts I wish I didn't have. The only thing that I knew for sure was that there wasn't anything I could do until it would happen again.

***

Sorry to say, but what Paul had said planted the bug in my brain, and I started paying closer attention to what Ri was doing and what she said she was doing. Several times over the next year, I followed her to see if she did anything that she shouldn't be doing. I told myself that if she was cheating with this Daniel when he came to town, why wouldn't she cheat when he wasn't around? Once a cheater, always a cheater, right?

Every couple of weeks she would stop after work for drinks with her co-workers and I followed her a few times and all she did was have one or two drinks and then go home. She never once danced with any of the men there or spent much time talking with anyone of them in particular. Maybe half a dozen times, I was outside her workplace around lunch time to see if she left work with anybody to catch a 'nooner' and she never did, at least not on the days I was watching.

I saw absolutely nothing to indicate that my wife was unfaithful and I had to conclude that either Ri was not cheating and Paul had been pulling my chain or Paul was telling the truth and she only cheated with this Daniel when he came to town,

***

It was just a tad over a year from when I had met Paul that I got my chance to find out what the truth might be. One night over dinner, Ri said:

"I've got another special project coming up next week so don't make any plans that will include me."

"Why don't they schedule those damned things far enough out so that people can plan around them?"

"It isn't my company that sets the deadlines, honey. The client calls, tells us what they want or need and when they have to have it and we have to respond. Believe me, honey, I really would like more notice about these things than I get."

Wednesday morning before I left for work, Adrianna reminded me that she would probably be working late that night.

"The good news is that we should be done by Friday night so I shouldn't have to work any this weekend."

"Well, at least that's something. Maybe we can go to the lake this weekend."

"That sounds like a marvelous idea."

She gave me a big kiss and said, "There, that should hold you until I get home. If you are still up, you might get more."

I was up when she got home. Not because I was horny and wanted to get laid, but because I wanted to make love to her and see if I could tell whether or not she might have already been laid. If she had, I couldn't tell. She didn't feel any different or act any different. The only thing I noticed was a faint scent that I didn't recognize. I wondered what it could be and then it occurred to me that it might be the scent of the soap used by the hotel or motel. But then maybe it could be the smell of someone she brushed up against in a crowded elevator. After all, she did work on the tenth floor of a tall building.

What is it that they say? That denial is a river in Egypt?

Well, any denial on my part that my wife would cheat on me was dispelled at the two-fifteen meeting I had with David Sloan of the Morresy Security and Investigative Agency.

"Subject left her place of employment at 4:32 PM and proceeded to walk two blocks to the Starburst Lounge. The subject entered the lounge and proceeded to a booth in the rear of the room. The subject was greeted by a male later ascertained to be one Daniel Martin. The subject and Mr. Martin hugged and kissed each other, sat down in the booth, and had one drink before getting up to leave. They left the Starburst and proceeded across the street to Hilton hotel where they took the elevator to the fourth floor where Mr. Martin had a room. The subject entered room 412 at 5:10 PM and remained in the room until 10:20 PM. When subject left the room, she was followed until she reached her residence at which time the surveillance was discontinued for the night."

Well, there it was. Paul hadn't lied. I made some arrangements with the detectives and then returned to work. I didn't get much done. I sat there and contemplated my marriage. It had been an extremely good one. I had been very happy with Ri and she had given every indication of being happy with me. Lord knows she did spoil me rotten. I was at a complete loss to understand how she could show me so much love and affection and then do what she was doing. I didn't know if the marriage could survive, but I did know that I was going to do whatever I could to try and save it.

***

I left work at three forty-five and went to the Hilton. I checked out the layout and saw which rooms would give me the best shot at what I planned on doing and then went down to the desk and asked if room 415 was available. I told the clerk that I tried to stay in that room every time I was in town since that was the room where I spent the first night when I married my wife. Luckily, it was open so I signed in and went up to the room and settled in.

At four forty-five, the detective called me on my cell and told me that the happy couple were on the way. I cracked the door a hair, and when I heard the elevator ding, I looked through the crack to see Adrianna and Martin coming down the hall hand in hand. I closed the door and moved to the bed and turned on the TV.

Figuring that the timeline for the night would be the same as the previous, I shut off the TV at five after ten and then cracked my door and took a seat next to it. At ten fifteen, I heard the door of 412 open, and through the crack I saw Adrianna heading down the hall to the elevator. When I heard the ping of the elevator door opening, I left the room and crossed the hall to 412. I knocked on the door gambling that he would open the door thinking that it was Adrianna coming back because she forgot something or remembered something she had to tell him or ask him.

The door started to open and I rammed it hard with my shoulder. The door slammed into him and sent him stumbling backwards, and I entered the room and was on him before he could catch his balance. I was wearing a pair of leather work gloves to protect my hands and I proceeded to beat the living shit out of him. I worked on him until he was on the floor groaning and then I kicked him hard ten or twelve times. I think I broke a rib or two and I know that his stones were going to take a long time to recover.

He was in a bathrobe and his clothes were folded and lying on a chair. I went over and got his wallet out of his pants. I dumped the contents on the table and went through them. I copied down all of the information on his driver's license. As I was doing that, I noticed him struggling trying to get up so I went over and kicked him in the head and he went back down. I went back to going through his wallet and I found a picture of a very beautiful woman with two kids. I put the picture in my pocket.

I went back over to him and drag him over to the bathtub and horsed him into it and then turned on the shower full cold. I ran cold water on him until he was aware enough to hear me.

"Are you right or left handed?"

"What?" he mumbled.

"Easy enough question. Are you right or left handed?"

"Why? What are you doing?"

"I want to know which arm to break."

"Go away," he whined, "I'm hurt. I need a doctor."

"You aren't hurting enough as far as I'm concerned. I'm giving my hands a rest before I start pounding on you some more. After which I'm going to break your arm and then you can go see a doctor."

He started to push himself up and I backhanded him and his head went back and banged into the wall. He slid back down into the tub and I said:

"You aren't going anywhere, Daniel, at least not until I am through with you."

He sniffed and whined. "Why are you doing this to me? I don't even know you."

"No, but you know my wife and in fact, you know her a lot better than I'm happy with."

"Your wife?"

"Oh come on, Daniel, you can't have forgotten her already. She's only been gone from here for about twenty minutes."

I saw the understanding take place across his face and then a trace of fear in his eyes.

"Here's the thing, Daniel. I have this ingrained thing about violence toward women. It is just something that I can't do, but I have all of this pent-up rage inside of me over what the two of you have been doing to me, and it has to come out. Since I just can't hit a woman, I can't touch Adrianna; therefore, you have to take the full brunt of my anger. Surely you can understand that. Now, back to my question. Are you right or left handed? Because even though I'm extremely pissed at you right now I still want you to be able to feed yourself and brush your teeth. That will make you appreciate your arms that much more which will in turn make you to not ever want to have both of them broken at the same time, and that is what will happen to you if you ever speak to Adrianna again. Now, which arm?"

"Please, man, no. Don't hurt me anymore. I won't ever see her or talk to her again. I swear it."

"I don't know, Daniel. You have caused me a lot of hurt, and I feel the crying need to get back at you."

I took the picture of the women with the two kids out of my pocket and showed it to him.

"How about instead of breaking an arm, I'll get on an airplane and fly to Akron? While I'm there, I can stop by 543 Meyers Court and pay this lady and the two kids a visit and share with them the anger I have over what you have been doing with my wife."

"Oh, man, God no. Please don't do that. It would kill her."

"Yes, but then she would have a whole lot of anger and she would take it out on you and really, Daniel. That is what this is all about. Making you suffer."

"No, man, come on, please. Please leave her out of this. Go ahead and break my arm, but please leave her out of this."

"You would take a broken arm to keep your wife from suffering? Maybe you do have a redeeming quality or two. Tell you what I'll do, Daniel. I'll settle for what I've already done to you, but there is a price. You agree to it and I'll get up and leave, your wife will never know and you won't suffer any more physical damage."

"I'll pay it. I'll do it. Whatever it is I'll do it just please leave my wife out of it."

"Okay, but you need to understand that if you backslide on the deal, your wife finds out everything and in addition I'll put you in a wheel chair. You understand?"

"I told you I'll do it. I promise. I'll do it."

"Okay, Daniel, here is the deal. You will never see Adrianna again. You will never speak to her again. You will not email her, send her a letter or a postcard or a smoke signal. There will be absolutely no contact between the two of you ever again. Are we clear on that?"

"Yes. I understand."

"One more time. No contact in any way, shape, matter, or form. If she calls you, you will immediately hang up without speaking a word to her. If she sends you an email, you will instantly delete it without reading it. If you get a letter, you will toss it in the wastebasket without opening it. If she approaches you on the street, you will turn and run— not walk, Daniel, but run—in the opposite direction. And lastly, she will never know we had this little talk. Are we clear on all of this?"

"Yes, sir. Perfectly clear."

"You need to know that I will be watching and if I catch even a hint that you are not living up to your end, I will know. Just like I knew about last night and tonight. I'll know and I promise you that if you ever see me again, it will not be in the least pleasant."

I got up and left his room. I knew that he could call the cops, but then his wife would find out and it seemed that he did not want that.

***

When I got home, Ri was waiting up for me. "Where have you been? I was worried when I got home and you weren't here and I couldn't reach you on your cell."

"Something came up at work and I had to work late. I drove over to your office to meet you so we could stop somewhere for a drink before we came home, but all the lights were off so I guessed that you had already headed home."

I saw something in her eyes when I said that, and I'm guessing it was something like "Oh shit!" but then the look changed to something that was probably a relief as she realized she had just dodged a bullet.

That night she was as passionate as always and I wondered at it. It didn't matter if Daniel was in town or not the level of her passion was always the same. She always behaved as if she couldn't get enough. I fell asleep wondering if I had solved the problem.

The next night Ri was home by seven and when I told her I hadn't expected her for hours she told me that things had all come together and they finished quicker than they expected. The others wanted to go out and have a drink or two to celebrate, but she begged off.

"I'd much rather be at home with you."

I got the story the next day when the detective called with his report. Daniel had checked out at eight, caught the hotel shuttle to the airport where he boarded the 10:10 flight to Akron. He was walking with a limp and seemed to be favoring his right side.

Adrianna got off work at her regular time and walked over to the lounge. Daniel wasn't there so she sat down and ordered a drink while she waited for him. After twenty minutes, she took out her cell and made a call but apparently got no answer. Fifteen minutes later, she tried the phone again, but still didn't talk to anyone. She waited another ten minutes and then she walked over to the hotel. She used the house phone to make a call and didn't get an answer so she walked over the desk and spoke to the clerk and found out that Mr. Martin had checked out. She went back to the lounge, had one more drink and tried her cell twice more, and then she had come home.

*** 

It has been a little over eight years now and during that time Ri has not had to work any special projects that cause her to work late or on the weekends. I keep a pretty close eye on her and she has done nothing to make me even slightly suspicious. She still spoils me rotten and tries to fuck me to death three or four times a week.

Maybe someday when we are old and gray, I might ask her about Daniel and her relationship with him and depending on my mood and the situation I might even tell her how I ended it.

**The End**

# The Project

She was hot! She was hot and she knew it. The table had been a "guy central" as guy after guy made the pilgrimage to the shrine to ask for her to bestow even the smallest amount of attention on them. She danced with a few, but turned three times as many away.

Some things never change.

***

She was hot! She was hot and she knew it. The two girls with her weren't bad, but they didn't even come close to her. A steady stream of guys made their way to her table and after a moment or two of conversation, she sent them on their way. Football players, baseball players, and all of the other types of jocks wanted to sit with her in her table in the school cafeteria, but she turned them all away.

I sat and watched and wished I had the nerve to try, but if she wouldn't have anything to do with the school's elite, what chance did a bookworm like me have. *None*, I thought, *not a chance in hell.*

Bobby the bookworm. That was me. The kid with the worst case of acne on the planet. The kid who sat in the back of the classroom. The shy guy who kept to himself.

***

Two years went by and Bobby the bookworm had filled out some. The acne had faded, but my face was so covered with scars and pits that it looked like a golfer with spiked shoes had walked across it. I was still the shy guy and I still sat in the school cafeteria and looked across the room to the table where she sat with her two friends and held court.

And then the strangest thing happened. She looked my way, our eyes met, and she smiled at me. I knew it as sure as I knew my own name. She didn't smile in my direction, she wasn't smiling as she looked off into space—she was smiling at me. The buzzer rang, announcing the end of lunch period and breaking the spell, and we all got up and shuffled off to our next class. I didn't have any shared classes with her in the afternoon so I didn't see her again until my first two classes the next day. I thought I saw her glance my way once or twice, but I was probably mistaken.

I was sitting in the cafeteria alone at a table which is how it usually was when she and her two friends came through the serving line. I, along with every other male in the place, watched as she paid the cashier. Next, she looked around for an empty table and we all watched as she and her two friends walked to it. It was the walk that we all wanted to watch. It was the sexiest sight in the world. Even if you couldn't see the rest of the package, the walk alone would give you the hard on of all hard ons.

The cashier gave her, her change and she looked around the room. There were several empty tables on the east side of the room and none on the side where I was sitting, although there were three empty seats at my table. She turned and headed toward the empty seats in my table and behind her I saw her two friends look at each other in confusion before following along behind her. She walked towards my table, looked at me, and said:

"May we join you?"

I was too stunned to say a word, but she knew that the likelihood of me saying no was on a par with the moon being found to really be a big blob of cheese, and so she sat down. She looked at me and said:

"Robert, right?"

I nodded a "yes".

"So tell me, Robert, why do you sit here every lunch hour and watch me like a hawk?"

Her friends looked from her to me and then back to her and "what the hell is going on here" was as clear on their faces as it was in my mind. I was shy, but it was the kind of shyness that prevented me from approaching people, not the tongue-tied kind of shy when people started talking to me. I smiled and said:

"Beauty attracts the eye. Extreme beauty attracts the eye and holds it."

She appeared surprised with that. The doofus was not a slack-jawed clown? I had no idea what she was thinking at that moment. I wasn't the kind of guy who was privy to the way a goddess would think. She gave me a dazzling smile and asked:

"If that is true, why have you never come over to talk to us?"

"What? Me? A commoner approach the throne?"

She laughed and said, "We could stand a steady diet of that kind of flattery, right, girls?"

Her two friends, Carol and Bev, gave half-assed smiles that clearly indicated that they had no idea of what was going on.

"Seriously," she said, "why haven't you ever spoke to me before?"

"I can turn that back on you. We have been classmates for over three years now. Why haven't you ever spoken to me?"

"Because I am the queen bee and all the males are supposed to approach me, not I them." And then she laughed and said, "The truth of the matter is that I have been pretty much a superficial stuck up twit. I'm so used to all of the good-looking guys fawning over me that I have never paid much attention to guys who look like you."

There was a sharp intake of breath from Bev and Carol when she said that and she laughed again and said:

"I'm the queen and the queen can say what she likes." She looked me right in the eye and said, "You know what you look like so you are not surprised that I see you the same way, right?"

I shrugged and said, "No, not really."

"Good. We start off with no illusions."

"Start off?"

"That's right, bubba, start off. Meet me after school and you can carry my books home."

"Carry your books?"

"A figure of speech, Robert. I usually go out the east door."

Then she switched subjects to who to vote for the prom king and queen and we talked while we ate lunch. When the buzzer went off, she said:

"East door at three. See you there."

She walked off, leaving me sitting there wondering what the hell had just happened. Befuddled, yes, stupid, no! At three I was on the steps outside the east door when she came out. Bev and Carol were with her and when they saw me waiting, I saw the look that passed between them. Each was soundlessly asking the other, "Do you know what is going on here?" There was no surprise on her face when she saw me because she knew that I would be there.

She handed me her book bag and I took it. At the bottom of the stairs, she turned right, but I took her arm and steered her to the left. She gave me a questioning look and I said:

"Bear with me, my queen. All will become clear soon."

I walked us into the student parking lot and up to a 1993 Ford Mustang convertible. I unlocked the passenger door, opened it as I bowed low and said:

"Your chariot awaits, my queen."

None of the three had ever seen the car before which wasn't all that odd since I'd never seen it myself before the previous night. It was my eighteenth birthday but the decision had been made that we would celebrate it on Saturday so I wasn't expecting anything until then. Mom had told me to take out the trash while she got dinner ready and dad got out the plates and utensils to set the table. I went out the door to the attached garage, where the garbage cans were, and stopped in my tracks when I saw the Sea Green Mist Mustang with white convertible top. It had a huge red bow on it and a streamer that said, "Happy Birthday, Rob."

I just stood there and stared at it. Mom and Dad came up behind me. Mom said, "Happy birthday, honey"; and my dad said, "The color is kind of yucky, but you're young enough that it can grow on you."

Mom punched him and said, "Shut up, you. It is beautiful and I'm pissed that you didn't give it to me and give Rob my clunky looking van."

"Couldn't give it to you," Dad said. "You go out driving in that and I'd be beating guys off of you with a stick and I'm too old for that shit."

Mom laughed and said, "You are kind of old and decrepit. Maybe Rob will loan it to me some night and I can go cruising and find me some stud who can keep up with me."

Dad said, "I'll show you old and decrepit." And he picked her up, put her over his shoulder, and carried her in the direction of the bedroom as she laughed and told him to put her down.

I held the door so Bev and Carol could get in the back and then she climbed in the front and settled into the white leather seat while I put the top down. I started it up and turned to her and said:

"Where would my queen like to go?"

That was the start of my relationship with Mellissa Anne Courtney.

***

She directed me to Bev's house and then to Carol's and told them that she would call them later. Once we were alone, she said:

"Why don't we go through the drive-thru, get a couple of Cokes, and then drive over to the park?"

"I hear and obey, my queen."

She laughed and said, "I should have found you sooner."

"I've been here all along."

"Tell me about yourself."

"Nothing to tell. I'm a bit shy and I keep mostly to myself, except for a half dozen really good friends. Mostly I go to school, study, and spend time at the library three or four times a week."

"Why so much time at the library?"

"I belong to a chess club that meets there on Tuesdays and a book discussion group that meets there on Thursdays. On Wednesdays, I read books to a group of four, five, and six year olds."

"I notice that you don't participate in any sports."

"Don't care much for them. I'm not into physical competition. I do play tennis with my mom on weekends and bowl with my dad sometimes, but I get most of my exercise in the gym that my dad set up in our basement. But enough about me. Why has the queen deemed this lowly commoner worthy of her attention?"

She was silent for a moment and just as she was getting ready to say something, we arrived at Burger Barn and pulled into the drive thru. I ordered two value meals and then drove across the street to the park, got out, and went to a picnic table and sat down. She took a bite of her burger and a sip of her Coke and then said:

"The truth hurts, Robert, but given the way you accepted my comment on your looks, I believe you can handle it. I also said that I was a superficial, stuck-up twit, and it is true, but I had never been aware of it. I didn't have to be because I was too busy being adored and fawned over. Boys have been flocking to me since I was twelve and I had my pick. If the one I picked turned out to be a toad, so what? Just dump him and pick another.

"I never lacked for a date and I didn't have a care in the world and it might have gone on that way forever if I hadn't overheard a conversation between my mom and dad. I wasn't supposed to be in the house. I was supposed to be at a sleepover at Carol's, but she got sick and so I went home. Apparently my parents didn't hear me come in, and they were talking about me. My dad was worried about my future if I didn't change my ways. He commented that all of my boyfriends were empty-headed jocks and if you took the last five I'd gone out with and lumped all their brains together, they still wouldn't be able to come up with the sense that God gave a grape. He said that the only reason that any of them spent any time at all studying was because they had to maintain an average of C or they couldn't play sports.

"My mom said it wasn't really that bad and besides, I was young and having fun like you were supposed to when you were my age. My dad said that was true, but he was afraid I'd take my taste in boys with me when I went off to college this fall and I'd end up with some meathead whose only ambition was to play pro ball.

"I went up to my room and thought about what he'd said and I realized he was right. The only guys I had ever dated were good-looking jocks. A lot weren't as dumb as my dad depicted, but they were almost all interested in sports and it seemed like that was all they talked about. When I studied, it was never with the guy I was dating at the time. I was always with Bev, Carol, or a couple of other girl friends. I tried to remember the last time I'd had a meaningful conversation with one of my boyfriends and I couldn't remember even one. My dad was right. I picked my boyfriends on appearance alone and it dawned on me that the reason I went through boyfriends so fast was that except for looks, they didn't have anything going for them that would capture and hold my interest.

"I thought about it for a couple of days and decided that I needed to see how the other half was. I looked around and there you were. This is the truth-may-hurt part. I wanted to get away from jocks. I wanted to get away from yummy-looking hunks. I wanted someone who my daddy wouldn't think of as just another meathead and like I said, there you were. Even at that, you were the luck of the draw.

"It was the night before last that I finally decided to do it, and I spotted you yesterday sitting alone at lunch and I thought, 'Whoa, Lissa, there he is, the perfect guy. Not the best looking and not a jock and he is on the honor roll every semester.' So when I saw you sitting alone at lunch today I headed for your table and here we are. So what do you think of your queen now?"

"So I am a social experiment?"

"Why don't we say that you are part of a project?"

"A project?"

"Yes. The project is to try and change the self-important, stuck-up superficial twit into something else. Are you up to the task?"

"Probably not."

She lifted an eyebrow at that and I said, "You said it yourself about four hours ago when you told me that you never paid much attention to guys who looked like me. The problem is that you are not the only girl with that attitude. I'm eighteen, and I have never been on a date with a girl and not from the lack of trying. I wouldn't have a clue as to what I could help you do as part of your project."

"You are pulling my leg, right?"

"Not in the least. Never found a girl who wanted to go out with a guy whose face looked like it had been worked over by a cheese grater."

She sighed and shook her head. "Last week, Mellissa would have been one of them. I guess there are two projects to work on now."

"Two projects?"

"Yep. Me and you. You get to work on the re-invent Mellissa project and I get to work on the turn Robert into a social butterfly project. Maybe they will complement each other. Can you dance?"

"My mom made me take dance lessons when I was in the seventh grade."

"Done any since then?"

"With my mom at home. She and my dad used to compete in ballroom dancing events. When he goes on business trips she wants to dance to fill in her evenings."

"Okay then. The first step in what I shall refer to as the "Bobby

Project" will be to get you out in the company of others on dates. The goal will be to have you ready to shine at the prom."

"The prom? I don't have a date for the prom. I don't even know anyone I can ask to the prom. Every girl I have ever asked for a date has turned me down."

"Of course you have a date, silly. You just haven't formally asked me yet."

"You? You are going to be my prom date?"

"Depends."

"On what?"

"A silly little requirement known as asking."

I looked at her, stunned, and she said, "Repeat after me, Robert. Will you go to the prom with me, Mellissa?"

I stared at her in total confusion. How could this be happening? The idea that the best-looking and most popular girl in school was sitting on a park bench and talking with me was mind boggling in itself. That she was telling me to ask her to the prom defied all logic.

"Come on, Robert, you can do it. Just follow me. Will you go to the prom with me, Mellissa?"

I pinched myself and felt the pain so I knew it wasn't a dream. I took a breath and asked:

"Miss Courtney, would you do me the honor of allowing me to be your escort to the senior prom?"

"I thought you would never ask. Of course, I will. Now that we have that settled, we need to go and see your mother."

"My mom? Why?"

"If she competed in ballroom dancing competitions, she knows how important it is for you to be in sync with your partner. We need to have her see us together so she can make comments and suggestions. As you point out, Robert, I am the queen and the queen will need to reign supreme on the floor at the prom. When would be a good time?"

"I'll have to ask when I get home."

She looked at me and I found that she was pretty good at reading facial expressions.

"What are you thinking, Robert?"

"I find it hard to believe that this close to the prom, the best-looking and most popular girl in the senior class doesn't already have a date, but mostly I find it hard to believe that you want to go to the prom with me."

"I have been asked by a half dozen guys and I have put them off since I was having a hard time trying to pick among them. I've already told you why I've never dated any one guy for very long and all the guys who asked me were the same as the ones I kept changing. There were all cut from the same cloth, out of the same mold so to speak. Your senior prom is supposed to be special and I was hoping for something better to come along. Then I did the re-evaluation thing and here we are. As your queen, I'm going to lay a quest on you. It is up to you to see that your queen's senior prom is special. Accomplish this and your queen may grant you a knighthood or kiss you and turn you from a frog into a prince. Fail your queen and she may leave you a frog forever."

"I hear and obey, my queen."

She laughed. "You big doofus. I should have checked out frogs sooner."

I drove her home and walked her to her door. She kissed my cheek and told me she would see me at school the next day.

Over dinner, I told my mom that I had a date for the prom and told her what Mellissa said about getting some pointers on our dancing, and mom told me to bring her home with me after school. I called Mellissa and she told me that she had no plans for that afternoon and that she was looking forward to dancing with me.

*** 

Mellissa and I shared two classes, and they were both in the morning. At the end of the second one, she told me to make sure that I saved her a seat in my table during lunch. When I sat down in the cafeteria, I thought I saw people looking at me and I wondered what was up with that.

I found out when Mellissa and the ever present Bev and Carol joined me at my table. Mellissa had told the guys who had asked her out that she wouldn't be going to the prom with them. She told Carol, Bev, and a few others that she was going with me and the school grapevine spread the word. After some small talk about what Mr. Anders had covered in the third hour, Mellissa asked me if it would be all right if Carol and Bev would come with her to my house and I said that it was okay with me.

At three I was waiting for them at the east door and we drove to my house. Mom and Mellissa seemed to instantly connect and after a bit of conversation mom said:

"Okay, you two, let me see what you got."

We went into the family room which had a hardwood floor. Mom puts on the CD that we usually danced to and started its playing. The first number was a waltz and it became immediately apparent that Mellissa couldn't dance. I mean she could dance like most teenagers, but she wasn't up to ballroom dancing standards. I was making her look bad. Not at all what I wanted for my queen. Mom was not the soul of discretion. She flatly told Mellissa:

"You need some work, honey. Let me show you what it should look like."

She held out here hand to me and hit the play button again, and I took mom around the floor until the tune ended. Then mom said:

"We need to do one of two things here. Either Bobby has to tone it way down or we need to bring you up."

Mellissa said, "I vote for bringing me up. How do I do it?"

"Hard work, honey. Hard work and time. How much can you give me?"

"Every minute I'm not in school. That includes weekends."

"What do we have? Two weeks until prom?"

Mellissa nodded a "yes."

"Okay then. Every night after school and all day on Saturday. If we make good progress we can skip Sundays." She turned to me and said, "It means that you will be responsible for having dinner ready when your dad gets home. That's all right with you?"

"No problem."

Mellissa said, "He cooks too?"

"My Bobby is a man of many talents. Sooner or later some very lucky young lady is going to realize what a catch he is."

I blushed and mom told me I wouldn't be needed for the day's lesson, but to be prepared to work hard the next day. As I headed for the kitchen I heard Bev ask if she and Carol could sit in. I didn't hear what mom said, but I was pretty sure it would be okay with her.

As I drove the girl's home, they talked about dresses and other prom-related things and when I got Mellissa home I walked her to her door. I got another kiss on the cheek and she told me to remember to save her a seat in my table the next day.

I was late getting to lunch the next day and when I got there Mellissa, Carol, and Bev were already at a table, but the fourth seat was occupied by Ray Hendricks so I found a seat on the other side of the cafeteria. That afternoon at three, Mellissa showed up at the east door alone and as we drove to my house, she apologized for not saving me a seat at the table.

"Ray sat down before I could tell him that I was saving the seat for you. He started talking to Bev about their prom date so I couldn't chase him away."

I shrugged and we pulled into my driveway. We were just walking into the house when I found out why Carol and Bev hadn't been with Mellissa when she came out of school. Ray pulled up in front of the house and he and Bev got out of his car even as Carol and Steve Miller pulled up behind him. I looked at Mellissa.

"Your mom said she would also work with Bev and Carol and their dates."

I just shrugged and said, "I guess the queen's court should look good too," and we went into the house.

Mom was in her element. She had to be a dance instructor just waiting to come out of the closet. She spent the afternoon going through the basics using me as a visual aid until about and hour before Dad was due home and then I had to hit the kitchen and start fixing dinner. When Dad got home, he worked with mom on the lesson and around six thirty, things broke up and mom came and told me that Mellissa was staying for dinner.

Dad pretty much dominated the dinner table conversation asking Mellissa all about herself, her family, what she was going to study in college and what were her goals in life. When dinner was over, he said he would handle the clean up so I could work with Mom and Mellissa. At nine, I drove Mellissa home and as soon as we pulled away from my house, she said:

"Okay, Robert, give."

"What?"

"Why the long face earlier when Ray and Steve showed up with Bev and Carol?"

I was silent for a moment and then said, "I've spent most of my school years with girls having little or nothing to do with me and then my fairy godmother took pity on me and waved her magic wand. The fairy dust settled and there you were. That is the only possible explanation for it. And like when the fairy godmother only gave Cinderella until midnight, I know that I am only going to have a short time with you and I guess I don't want to share what little time I will have with anyone else."

She didn't say anything to that, but then what could she say? She knew it was true. I walked her to her door and she turned to face me with a strange look on her face as she said she would see me at school the next day. She leaned forward and kissed me. Not on the cheek, but on the lips. Then she turned and went inside.

When I got home Dad said that he would order pizza for the next day's dinner and then take over the kitchen chores on Saturday to give me more time to work with Mellissa.

"I think you got a good one there, sport, and we need to do what we can to see to it that you keep her."

"Yeah right," I thought. Like that could ever happen.

*** 

Friday at lunch, all the talk was about dancing and prom dresses and my only part of the conversation came when I was asked what dances I thought were likely to be played. I said it was more likely that half would be waltzes and the rest fast numbers based on current popular tunes, and I speculated that there would be at least one each for tango, cha-cha, and samba.

"Do we have time to learn those?" Carol asked.

"Maybe some of the basics," I replied.

Of course that night, Carol had to bring it up, and equally, of course, mom took it as a challenge.

"How hard do you want to work?" she asked. "We can work late tonight and then a full day tomorrow. You will need to be here Sunday most of the day and next week work a couple of hours later than we have been. We have tonight, all of this weekend and all of next week and weekend. I think we can do it, but you won't have time for much else."

I could tell that Ray and Steve were not all that interested in doing it, but Mellissa, Carol, and Bev were all for it so Ray and Steve got dragged along. It was either that or possibly losing girlfriends thirteen days before the prom. We worked until ten before calling it a night and then I took Mellissa home. We were almost to Mellissa's house when she said:

"Your queen is pissed."

"And what pray tell has this lowly one done to upset his queen?"

"We haven't been on a date yet. We have spent all this time together and have yet to go on a date."

"This lowly one apologizes, but at the risk of incurring the wrath of his queen he must say that it was the queen who made the decision to fill up all of her available time with dance lessons."

She looked at me for a moment before saying, "I guess I did, didn't I?"

Before I got to her house, she told me to take a left on Jerry Street.

"Why are we doing that?"

"Be patient. You'll see."

She had me make a right on Paris and I looked questioningly at her because Paris was a dead end. At the end of the block she told me to pull over and park. I did as she said and then she said, "Get in the back," as she got out on her side and moved to the back and I followed.

"It doesn't look like we are going to be able to squeeze in a date before prom and I'll be damned if I'm going to wait thirteen more days to do this. We can't do it up front because of the bucket seats, center console, and gear shift so we will have to do it back here. Kiss me."

I was going to argue? She broke the kiss and said, "You weren't joking when you said there hadn't been any girls in your life were you? If there were, they sure didn't teach you how to kiss. Here, let me show you."

And she did. After a couple of minutes she said, "Not bad, but we will have to spend some time working on it." And then she sought my lips again. It was another half hour before she told me that it was time for me to get her home. The goodnight kiss at her front door was a little on the intense side and I drove home giving my fairy godmother effusive thanks. It might not last long, but I was going to have some very nice memories.

***

The next ten days took on a sameness. We spent twelve hours a day on Saturday and Sunday working under the task master that my mother had become. Monday through Friday was school and then after school four more hours of lessons. The following Saturday and Sunday were also twelve hour days. Each night when I drove Mellissa home there was a make-out session. Sometimes I got the feeling that Mellissa was waiting for me to do something, but I didn't know what.

When I got home after taking Mellissa home following Sunday's session, mom told me that she thought that Mellissa and I were almost good enough for competition.

"You've always been ready, baby, but Mell does need just a little more work. Carol would be too if she had a better partner, but I'm sorry to say that Bev and Ray don't have what it takes. They will shine at the prom, but that will be because most of the other kids won't have had the benefit of lessons."

"You really think that we are that good together?"

"You bet, baby."

I went to bed that night feeling pretty damned good.

***

That good feeling was with me right up until the end of the fourth hour. At the end of our second-hour class, Carol asked me to meet her outside the east door before going to the cafeteria for lunch and then she took off for her next class without giving me a chance to ask why or even agree to meet her. Curiosity being what it is, I was there waiting when she came out. She walked up to me and hesitated. She wanted to say something, but it seemed she either didn't know what to say or how to say what she did want to say. I tried to help.

"Go ahead, Carol. As you might imagine I'm used to hearing bad things from girls. I can handle it."

She took a deep breath and then she said, "Mell is my best friend, and I usually don't butt into her business, but over the last couple of weeks I've discovered what a great guy you are and what a great family you have. I don't want to see you get hurt, Rob, but I'm afraid that Mell is going to hurt you. I know why she is spending time with you, but I know her Rob. I know that you aren't the kind of guy who will hold her interest for long. She is using you to satisfy some need she feels she has and then she will drop you like she has a dozen others.

"I see the way you look at her, Rob, and I know how you are going to feel when it happens. I guess I hoped if I prepared you for it that it might help some."

"I appreciate your concern, Carol, but I'll be okay. I've always known that it wouldn't last. At least I will have prom and that is something that wouldn't happen before Mellissa took an interest in me for whatever reason."

"That brings up the other thing. You do know that you will only be able to spend part of the prom with her right?"

"What do you mean?"

"She is bound to be elected prom queen and Dick Harbor will more than likely be named prom king and they will have to spend some time together. Then there is the queen's court and tradition says that she has to dance with all the male members of her court."

I shrugged and said, "At least in the record books, I would have been her date, and our picture will be in the class yearbook. That is something I'll always have. Come on, we're late for lunch."

That night after our dance lesson, I drove Mellissa home and as soon as I pulled out of the drive Mellissa said:

"I saw Carol talking to you today. What was that all about?"

I hesitated and she said, "Come on, sweetie, you can tell me. Carol and I are too tight for whatever you tell me to affect us."

"She says she likes me and doesn't want to see me hurt."

"So?"

"She more or less told me not to let myself get too close to you."

"Why would she do that?"

"The idea was that if I didn't get too close, it wouldn't hurt as bad when you dump me and move on to your next conquest."

"And you think that is going to happen?"

"Given my history with the opposite sex, why wouldn't I? You are the queen and I am a lowly serf, and we lowly serfs know better than to try and climb too high."

"Pull over."

"What?"

"Pull the fuck over!"

I'd never heard a profane word from her so I was shocked, but I did pull over next to the curb. She turned and climbed over the center console and shift lever, turned off the ignition, and then she kissed me. The kiss turned into a hot make-out session. She lifted her sweater, grabbed my right hand, and put it on her breast and then she placed one of her hands on my hard cock and rubbed it.

"I've never done this with any other guy. Not one of the studs and hunks I've dated have ever gotten this. You are special, Robert, and you are my guy. You are stuck with me, asshole, so get used to it!"

It was a nice thought for me to carry around even if I didn't believe it.

***

Tuesday and Wednesday went by quickly and it was prom night. My mom had picked out the corsage and she handed it to me as I started to leave. I was headed for the garage to get the Mustang when my dad said:

"Where are you going?"

"To get my car."

"Your ride is out in front."

I went to the front door and saw a stretch limousine sitting at the curb. He handed me two one-hundred-dollar bills and said, "Have fun." When I got to Mellissa's house and she came down the stairs to greet me, she was so beautiful that I almost lost my breath. If I didn't get to experience anything else, I at least got to see that vision walk toward me.

I had to pose for pictures as Mellissa's mom took twenty or thirty shots with her camera and she told me that she would make a set for my mom as I walked Mellissa to the door.

"You might want one of my queen getting into her chariot," I said as I opened the front door and Mellissa walked out onto the porch and saw the limo.

"Hopefully, it won't turn into a pumpkin before I get you home."

Mellissa turned and kissed me with a kiss that made me weak in the knees and her mother got a shot of it.

"Would you please make me a thousand copies of that one?" I asked and her mother laughed.

All eyes were on us as we walked in. Half of those watching were probably thinking "What the hell is she doing with him?" And most of the males present were drinking in her beauty and wishing they were me.

Mellissa, Carol, Bev, Ray, Steve, and I dazzled the rest of the attendees as we dipped and swirled around the floor. Mellissa was indeed installed as prom queen and Carol and Bev ended up as part of her court. The biggest surprise was that Dick Harbor didn't make it as king. The honor instead went to Mike Ashell who was one of Mellissa's old boyfriends.

The biggest shock of the night came when it was time for the king and queen to dance. Mike had this big grin on his face as he walked up to Mellissa while the band started playing a waltz. The smile disappeared when Mellissa reached up, took the crown off his head, walked over to me, placed it on my head and then led me out onto the dance floor.

Just the two of us, alone on the floor with every eye in the place on us. If we had been in a dance competition during that dance, we would have swept the floor with the other contestants. We were that good together. When the music finally stopped, Mellissa and I bowed to each other as the place erupted in thunderous applause. I found out later that the band leader played the waltz an extra three minutes because we were doing so well he didn't want to stop us.

Mellissa took the crown from my head and took it back to Mike and then led him out onto the floor for the next dance. Carol walked up to me, elbowed me in the ribs, and said:

"Show off. My turn now."

I danced with Carol, Bev, and several other girls that night because there was no way I could keep Mellissa to myself for the entire evening, but I did have her for more than half the night.

There were one or two other highlights. When the band played a cha-cha, mom's students were the only ones out on the floor, and when a half hour later they played a second one, mom's students each grabbed a partner from the crowd and led them out onto the floor and tried to lead them through the dance. The same thing happened when the band played two tangos. The first was just mom's crew and the second was mom's crew pulling partners from the crowd.

During the second tango, I pulled Nancy Neubert out onto the floor and as I tried to lead her through the dance, she said:

"Damn, Rob. Where the hell have you been hiding?"

I almost laughed in her face. I had asked her for a date at least a half dozen times since we were in ninth grade together and she had always shot me down. I just smiled and kept my mouth shut.

The last dance was a waltz and all was well with my world as I moved around the floor with Mellissa in my arms. As the last note faded, she kissed me and said:

"You are a frog no more, my prince."

\*\*\*

My reverie was broken as she sat down beside me.

"Having second thoughts?" she asked.

"Not at all. Just thinking back to the senior prom."

"I could tell. That's why I asked you if you were having second thoughts."

"Not a one. It was just a paving stone on the walkway that led us here."

"More like two or three."

"Want another drink?"

"I don't think so. I told the sitter we would be home by eleven."

"Okay. I just need to make a quick trip to the bathroom."

When I came out, I saw Mellissa talking to Carol. Carol said something and Mellissa laughed and then Bev said something and Mellissa laughed as Carol stuck out her tongue. They all hugged and I marveled at a friendship that had lasted for over eighteen years, from the sixth grade until now. I've had friends and good buddies galore, but I couldn't think of even one that I've been as close to as Mellissa, Bev, and Carol were to one other.

I walked up and put my arm around my wife. "Goodnight, all," I said as Carol and I turned and walked out of the Landing Strip Lounge and headed for home.

**The End**

# The Phony Excuse

Dave Valerta stared at his wife sitting across the room from him, stunned by what she had said. How could his wife of eighteen years and the mother of his children say something like that to him? "Don't look at me like that, Dave. It's your own damned fault."

It had happened the night of Diane's sister's birthday party. At the last minute, a problem had come up at the plant and Dave couldn't get away from work until the problem was solved. He had called Diane and told her she would have to go alone and that he would meet her there when he could get away. Diane had gone off on him because she was sure he was making a phony excuse so he could get out of going. It didn't help that he and Diane's sister couldn't stand each other and did their best to avoid being in the same place at the same time. But there wasn't much Dave could do about it. As production manager, he had to be there when there were production problems. It was past midnight when Dave finally left the plant and since he figured that it was way too late to go to Donna's party, he went on home. He was not surprised that Diane was not home yet. His parents had taken the kids for the weekend and Diane would stay at the party until the last dog was hung, if for no other reason than to spite Dave. He had gone to bed knowing that Saturday was going to be a bitch even if Diane didn't talk to him. She had a way of turning the house into a huge deep freeze when she was pissed.

When he'd awakened, Diane was not in bed with him. He checked the kid's rooms, the spare bedroom, and the living room couch and it was apparent that Diane had not come home. He figured that she must have spent the night at Donna's rather than try to drive home with a snoot full. Well, at least that would put off the confrontation a little while longer. He spent the morning changing the oil in his car and rotating the tires. When Diane still wasn't home by two, he decided that he better call Donna. Not that he was worried, but because he could already hear what Diane would say if he didn't. "You don't even care enough about me to try and find out if I'm alright." When Donna answered the phone and he'd asked to speak to Diane Donna had laughed at him, "She's not here, dickhead."

"What time did she leave?"

"About one last night."

"But she never came home."

"Might not have come home to you, but she went home with somebody. Not bad looking either, and she spent quite a bit of time swapping tongues with him before they left. Face it, dickhead, you've been replaced."

Donna's laughter rang in his head as she hung up on him. Diane had left the party with another man at one o'clock? That's the last thing that Dave would have expected from Diane and he had a very bad feeling about where his life was now headed.

It was seven thirty that evening when Diane's car pulled into the driveway. Dave was sitting in the kitchen, eating some leftovers that he'd fixed for himself when she walked in. He looked up at her briefly and then took his plate to the sink, rinsed it, and put it in the dishwasher. Then he took another brief look at Diane and walked out of the room. He went into the living room, turned on the TV, and settled in to watch the war news on CNN. Operation Iraqi Freedom seemed to have bogged down in a sandstorm. Diane came into the room and sat down in the easy chair across from him. "Aren't you even going to ask me where I've been?"

Dave hit the mute button on the TV. "I know where you've been. Your pig of a sister couldn't wait to tell me that you left the party with another man at one o'clock last night. Being a fairly intelligent person, it wasn't at all hard for me to figure out what you have been doing. Where you did it doesn't really matter now, does it?"

"It might not matter, but I'm going to tell you anyway. When you gave me that phony excuse about problems at the plant just so you could get out of taking me to Donna's party, I got mad. As the party went on and you never showed up. I got madder and madder and of course I had a lot to drink. Donna introduced me to one of the men she works with and we hit it off. The party started winding down and you still hadn't come and Stan asked me to have a drink with him. I followed him to a bar and we sat and talked until last call. I was having such a good time talking to him that when he invited me over to his place to finish the conversation I said yes. I wasn't going to do anything but sit and talk, but things got out of hand and I ended up letting him make love to me. I liked it. I liked it so much that I did it again, several times. He wants to see me again and I just might let him. Don't look at me like that, David, it's your own damned fault."

David stared at his wife in stunned disbelief at her statement that it was his fault that she was a cheating whore. "I would be interested in knowing how your being a cheating slut is my fault."

Diane winced at the word slut but Dave really didn't care about her feelings at that point.

"It's your fault for using that phony excuse to avoid my sister. If I hadn't been there alone and in a pissed off mood, it would never have happened."

"Is that it? You have anything else you want to say?" Diane shook her head "no" and Dave turned his attention back to the TV and clicked the mute button to get the sound back.

Diane said, "You seem to be taking this well."

"What to take? You cheated on me, which tells me that our marriage never meant shit to you. Okay, now I know and I can get on with my life."

"What do you mean?"

"I mean that I'll see a lawyer on Monday."

Diane got a panicked look on her face. "A lawyer, why?"

"You don't think that I'm going to stay married to a cheating whore, do you?"

"But I don't want a divorce, David. I love you and I want to be with you."

"You didn't want to be with me from one o'clock last night until fifteen minutes ago."

"It was a mistake, David. I'd been drinking. I was in a rotten mood. I was upset with you and things happened, and I'm sorry. I didn't mean to, David, I honestly didn't mean for it to happen."

"But it did happen, Diane. And when it happened, you didn't jump out of that asshole's bed, remorseful and guilt stricken, and run home hoping to save your marriage. You stayed there with the asshole for eighteen hours and then you came home and told me how much you enjoyed it. And then, if that wasn't bad enough, you tell me he wants to see you again and that you just might let him."

"I didn't mean it, honey, I was just trying to shake you up."

"Well, you did it, Diane. You managed to shake me right out of this marriage."

Dave got up and got the day's paper off of the coffee table and handed it to Diane. "My phony excuse is on page three." And then he watched Diane's face lose some color as she read about the power failure that shut down the XYZ Company and idled over one-hundred-thirty-five workers for over seven hours. "There is a bright side for both of us on this, Diane. You can call your sister and give her the good news that I'm out of your life now. The bright side for me is that I'll never have to see or talk to the bitch ever again. Call her now and after you give her the good news, ask her if she has room for you because you are not staying here with me. I'm not about to put up with the stink of your asshole lover."

"Please, David, don't do this to me."

"I didn't do it to you, Diane, you did it to yourself. Now live with it." And he left the room.

### The End

# The Personal Assistant

As I touched up my makeup in the ladies room, I thought about what was likely to happen when I went back to the table. No, that wasn't true—I knew what was going to happen—what I wondered about were the possible outcomes from what was going to happen. It wasn't every day that my boss asked me to take care of a large group of people, and I had to wonder why he thought that I would go along with it. Granted that I was letting him bed me even though I was a married woman, but that didn't make me a slut. Or did it? I guess that would be a matter of perspective. I didn't think of myself as a slut, but it was a good bet that my husband would, if he knew. I would just have to make sure that he never did.

*** 

Once upon a time I was a fairly boring housewife and mother who stayed at home and took care of the zoo. Then the kids grew up and suddenly I was looking at an empty nest. For the first month I was in heaven. No pressure and lots of free time for myself, and then I ran out of things to do around the house. I quickly found that nothing but a steady diet of daytime soaps would turn your brain to mush so I got off my buns and went out looking for a job.

It did not take long at all to realize those twenty-one years of being a stay-at-home wife and mother did not arm me with the skills that would translate into the current job market. After two weeks of steady looking, I had found nothing. Oh, there were jobs I could have gotten, convenience store clerk on the night shift for one, but I wasn't the least bit interested in stocking shelves at oh-dark-thirty or flipping burgers.

I'd just spent ten hours pounding the pavement, answering ads with no luck. My husband was out of town—again—and I was in no mood to hurry home to an empty house so I stopped at a lounge to enjoy a drink. The drink turned into three and then the waitress came over and told me that a gentleman at the bar wanted to buy me a drink.

"Do you know him? Is he really a gentleman or is he just trying to get lucky?"

She laughed and said, "I don't really know about the gentleman part, honey. He's in here two or three times a week and he has never caused any trouble, that's all I can say about him."

"Tell him I accept it," and then I did something totally out of character and added, "providing that he joins me."

As the waitress walked away, I wondered what in the world had possessed me to do that.

His name was Bob and the word that described him best was pleasant. He was pleasant looking, had a pleasant personality, and he was pleasant company. Not much for originality though. His opening after the name exchange was, "And what's a pretty girl like you doing all alone in a place like this?"

I almost laughed, but since I wasn't the least bit interested in letting myself be picked up but did want some company at the table, I behaved myself. We talked and had several more drinks as I explained to him the trials and tribulations of my job search.

"I can sympathize with you. I'm having as much trouble finding someone willing to work for me as you are trying to find a job."

My ears perked up when I heard that and he noticed and laughed, "No, I don't think so. You just are not the type."

"How do you know that? We just met and you don't know anything about me."

"I know you are married."

"What has that got to do with it? Just what is the job?"

"Personal assistant."

"You are probably right then. I haven't done any typing since high school."

"Personal assistants don't type. I have secretaries for that stuff."

"What does a personal assistant do?"

"Waits on me hand and foot. She takes care of all the little odds and ends that tend to clutter up an already too busy schedule. Follows along behind me with a pad and pen to make notes, remind of appointments and meetings, see to it that my dry cleaning gets sent out, make sure that I remember important birthdays and anniversaries, and take care of a whole host of other personal needs."

"Sounds like just what I have been doing for the last twenty years, waiting hand and foot on two kids and a husband. What does a job like that pay?"

"My last assistant was making eighty grand a year before her husband made her quit."

"What would make a man make his wife give up that kind of money? That's more than my husband makes."

"I guess he didn't like some facets of her job. She didn't mind them, but I guess her marriage mattered enough to her that she gave in to him."

"What facets of the job didn't he like?"

"She had to travel with me on business three or four times a month and I guess he got upset at some of the personal things she had to do."

"Hell, my husband travels more than that. He wouldn't even miss me because he would be on the road too. What personal things didn't her husband like?"

"Look, I'm a very busy man most of the time, and I don't have the time to take care of some things. One of the things that Mellisa did was to arrange some of my personal urges to be taken cared of."

"You mean she arranged sexual meetings for you? Found you women?"

"Sometimes."

"What does that mean?"

"Sometimes she couldn't find anyone."

Suddenly what he was saying dawned on me. "Oh, oh my. And her husband found out?"

"No, he just suspected, but it was enough to make her quit."

"Quitting a job that paid that much just because he was suspicious? If it were me he would damned well have had to know for sure before I'd give it up."

By that point it was the booze that was talking, not the real me, and when Bob said, "Are you telling me that you could take on a job like that?"

"For that kind of money? In a heartbeat!"

"Okay, let's get the job interview out of the way."

"What?"

"My office is just across the street. I want to get you over there and fill out the application before you sober up and chicken out."

It had to have been the liquor because I wasn't that kind of woman, or at least I didn't used to be, but five minutes after we entered his office he entered me. The surprising thing to me was that I didn't feel any guilt at cheating on my husband. Bob was the first man other than my husband to have me since the day of my wedding almost twenty-one years ago. It was sex at its most elemental. I was on my back on Bob's desk with my skirt up around my waist and the gusset of my panties pushed to the side to give him entrance. He did lose his trousers, but he still had his shirt, tie, shoes, and socks on. He banged away at me and I clutched his butt cheeks with my hands, wrapped my legs around him, and moaned in pleasure. I climaxed twice before he came and when it was over he said, "That is going to be part of your duties. Do you still want the job?"

I guess that deep inside me, there must have been some brazen hussy because I smiled and said, "I get that and money too? Hell yes, I want the job."

"Okay, you're hired."

He got up and put on his pants and then he picked up the phone.

"I'm ready, Paul." And then he walked back to me and offered me a hand to help me up. "Come on, my dear. You are on the payroll now and we have places to go and things to do."

There was a limo waiting at the curb when we walked out the front door and a uniformed chauffeur opened the rear door for us.

"Paul, this is Chrissi. She's my new PA. Chrissi, this is Paul and you will probably be spending an awful lot of time with him from now on. Give Paul your address."

"But my car is in the lounge parking lot."

"I'll arrange to have it taken cared of. You won't be needing it from now on. Paul will be picking you up at seven in the morning and bringing you home at night."

I was just a little bit surprised when he dismissed Paul when we got to my home. Bob saw my look.

"You did say he was out of town, right?"

I nodded a yes.

"Good. It gives me time to get to know you better."

That night I was treated to the unique and mind-blowing experience of sliding up and down on another man's hard cock while taking my husband's nightly check-in phone call. I couldn't explain what had happened in the four hours since I had met Bob, but I felt no guilt or remorse at cheating on Glenn. None! I loved Glenn dearly and I would die for the man if the need arose, but it didn't bother me one bit to fuck Bob.

The next morning Paul was waiting when Bob and I came out of the house at six forty-five and on the way to the office I got my rude awakening. You know the saying that if it sounds too good to be true, it is? Well, getting eighty thousand a year for being Bob's PA was too good to be true. Bob had said that when Mellisa had left, she was making that much, but that was her total with bonuses, commissions, and a few other things like a clothing allowance and company credit cards. The actual salary was four thousand a month, which was still very good money. I spent most of the day filling out forms for life and health insurance and all kinds of other stuff. Then I was turned over to Bob's secretary who sat me down and explain in great detail what I was supposed to do as Bob's personal assistant (she didn't say a word about the sex part) and then she handed me a list and three company credit cards and told me to take the rest of the day and purchase what was on the list.

"Experience has shown that you will need these items at one

time or another." And then she handed me a second list. "Have these items packed and ready to go because there are times you will be going out of town on a moment's notice and you won't have time to go home and pack."

I looked at both lists and saw that they were mostly clothes. A full-length evening gown for a formal affair, business suits, cocktail dresses, and the like.

"Try to have them all by tomorrow. Paul will drive you."

\*\*\*

That was almost six months ago, and probably the most surprising thing to me about the job, considering the way it got started, was that Bob did not require my sexual services all that much. Mostly it was when we were out of town on trips and the sex on those trips was intense. Bob usually wanted to go all night and we usually did. At home, we did occasionally have some two-martini lunches that ended up in a hotel room, but it was rare unless my husband was out of town on business. If that was the case, Bob would come over so he could be sliding his cock in me when I took my evening call from Glenn. For some reason, he got a major charge out of that (for that matter, I did too) and doing it on Glenn's bed.

Bob had a philosophy—work hard and then go play. His day started at five thirty and ended at six in the evening unless he had a dinner or some special event to attend. His theory was, "If you can't get it done in a twelve-hour day it doesn't need to be done."

But those twelve-hour days were non-stop and many nights when Paul dropped me off, all I wanted to do was soak my feet in the tub. A typical day for me started when Paul picked me up at seven. I had a cell phone that only one person—Bob—had the number, and between seven and five after seven it would ring and I would get my basic instructions for the start of the day.

"Set up an appointment with so and so. Must be before noon Friday. My tux is at the tailors being altered. Call them and tell them I must have it by three today and arrange to have it picked up. Call whatsis at XYZ and tell him I want his proposal no later than noon today. Don't let him messenger it, go and pick it up. My meeting with Billings is at nine thirty and I need him distracted so show a lot of leg while you are taking notes. A low-cut blouse wouldn't hurt either. Make sure that my schedule is clear from twelve thirty to two and reserve us a room at Hilton. I plan on fucking Billings during our negotiations and you know how horny that makes me. What have you got for me?"

I checked my Day-Timer. "You need to call your sister and wish her a happy birthday. Your yearly physical will be tomorrow at nine so no foods and nothing but water to drink after six tonight. You promised Baxter a call today about his inventory problem and, like it or not, you promised your ex you would talk to her today about your daughter's college plans."

"Shit! You know how much I hate hearing that bitch's name let alone having to talk with her. Oh well, I did promise. I'll see you when you get here."

How was my husband Glenn reacting to my new job? Amazed and stunned would be a pretty good description. Glenn had worked his butt off for twenty years to get to where he was making fifty-eight thousand a year and I go out and fall into a job that in six months had me almost making the same. My Christmas bonus from Bob was ten thousand and if I had worked for the full twelve months I would have made five thousand more than Glenn. Glenn certainly wasn't unhappy with the extra money coming in because it allowed him to splurge. We had lived comfortably on his income so my paycheck was like having a windfall. We bought a cabin on a lake, a boat and trailer and a Dodge Ram to pull it and started socking money away in the savings account.

Glenn isn't suspicious of anything that I was doing because he thought he knew exactly what it is. His boss has a PA and he pretty much sees what she does and the hours she puts in, but Sarah, while a beautiful person, is a mousy spinster type. There wasn't any way that Glenn could imagine her and Ralph getting it on so the thought that I might be doing more for Bob than Sarah does for Ralph just never occurs to him.

My hours and trips didn't bother him because of the traveling he does. We always had the weekends together and things seemed to be working out just fine for us. Our sex life was fantastic. The more I fucked Bob the more erotic and wicked I felt when I made love to Glenn. When he asked why the sudden increase in intensity, I told him about how Bob had me dress and sit so I would be a distraction to the men he did business with and that doing it made me all hot and horny and that I had to come home and take it out on him.

*** 

I never did get to where I felt guilt or remorse at hanging horns on Glenn. It was probably a flaw in my character. I loved Glenn to death and I would quit what I was doing in a heartbeat if it got to where it would cost me Glenn, but for the time being I was just having too much fun. I'd just have to work very hard at seeing that Glenn never had reason to get suspicious like Mellisa's husband did.

*** 

It was shortly after the company Christmas party that Bob asked me if I would be willing to put a little extra effort into seeing that a certain corporate account stayed with us. I'd wondered when or if this would ever come up and I had given it tons and tons of thought. Without Bob even asking, I knew what it was. It was how Mellisa, his last PA had earned so much more than I was currently making. He wanted to know if I would be willing to service a customer. The company grapevine had already told me that Mellisa got commissions for seeing that certain customers were kept happy and now it was my turn. As I said, I'd given the matter lots of thought and had pretty much made up my mind about what I would do if it was asked of me. The bottom line wasn't the commissions I might get, it was the job. I was in love with my job and I was afraid that if I said "no," my days would be numbered. Bob's PA took care of problems, this customer was a problem; ergo, the PA will handle it. So, as cheerily as I was able, I said, "When and where?"

It was surprisingly easy. Bob and I met the customer for lunch at Hilton, and after a leisurely lunch accompanied by several glasses of a very good wine, Bob excused himself to make some phone calls. I suggested to the customer that we go up to the company's hospitality suite and wait for Bob there. Five hours later and feeling like a slut, a very well used slut, Paul drove me home.

On the drive home, my eyes met Paul's in the rear view and I wondered if the grapevine had been right about him and Mellisa and how I would handle the situation if it ever came up. Paul was a very good-looking black man and I did have to admit to some curiosity about some of the things I had heard about black men. After that afternoon, I had to wonder if one more cock would matter. I had taken care of the customer—three times—and he had no sooner gone when the door to the suite opened and Bob came in undressing as he moved toward me. He shocked the hell out of me by going down to his knees and burying his face in my well-used pussy. He also fucked me three times before letting me go. I came to find out that Bob's biggest turn ons were sloppy seconds and what he called cream pies. He just loved sucking another man's cum out of my pussy and over the course of the next year, he got quite a bit of that from me.

\*\*\*

After that first time, Bob would ask me, on the average of twice a month, to "handle" a particular account; and I of course did and after each and every time, Bob would come into the room, eat my pussy, and then soak his cock in the other man's leavings. It was quite kinky and I soon got to the point where I got an erotic charge out of it. Just before Bob would come into the room, I would drag a finger through the mess and then suck the goo off my finger and roll it around in my mouth. Then Bob would come in and I would French kiss him as he entered me.

Once, I asked him why he never ate my pussy after I had fucked Glenn in the morning.

"You know my rule when it comes to business, sweetie, hit the ground running first thing in the morning, no time for sex until later in the day. Get Glenn to fuck you at lunch time and then come to me and I'll gladly do it."

I wondered if someday I could make it happen.

Bob had one other kink that also turned me on. He loved to have his cock in me when we were on a business trip and I was calling home to talk to my husband. At first I was terrified that I would moan or the bedsprings would squeak and that Glenn would hear and figure out what was happening, but I got over the fear and sometimes I got pretty aggressive sliding up and down on Bob's cock while telling Glenn how much I loved him and missed him. A couple of times, it was a customer's cock I was riding when I talked to Glenn and those times I had some intense orgasms.

Then Bob took me to the next step. One night on a trip, when I was supposed to take care of a customer, Bob stayed in the room with us. I had my first double penetration and I absolutely loved it. It gave me such a feeling of power to know that I had those two powerful businessmen at my beck and call and that I could get them to do anything. In reality it was just the other way round—they could, and did, get me to do anything. They turned me every which way but loose. My phone call to Glenn that night found me with a cock in my pussy and one up my butt. After that night there were more threesomes and a couple of foursomes, all on out of town trips, and I honestly looked forward to them.

Tonight would be very different. Tonight I would be crossing a Rubicon of sorts. It was an executive retreat and most of the company's high-ranking officers were in attendance and Bob had asked me to serve as "hostess" in the company's hospitality suite. This would be the first time I played with people that I worked with on a daily basis at the office. Up until then, it had always been a customer or a supplier and not someone I was in daily contact with. That and the fact that there were twelve of them would make this a very different night indeed.

One last look at my lipstick and I turned and headed back to the table and…

**The End**

# The Truth About Maggie

"Put it against the wall," I told the two guys who carried in the dresser.

I went back to hanging the pictures on the wall. Tom came in with two suitcases and asked me where I wanted them.

"Put them on the floor in front of the bed. When you bring in the stuff on hangers, just put them in the closet."

When I was finished with the pictures, I put the suitcases on the bed and then emptied them into the dresser drawers. Tom and the other two guys—Mike and Phil—brought in the rest of the boxes and I had them put the stuff in the closet. Phil handed me a travel case and said:

"This is the last of it."

I took the case from him and then told the three of them that I'd meet them at Murphy's Tavern in half an hour. I emptied the case and put the items on top of the dresser, arranged them neatly, and stepped back to look around. I moved a few items to give things a more uniform appearance and then took a look around the room. Satisfied with what I saw, I turned and left and went to meet my buddies at Murphy's.

\*\*\*

I was on my second beer when my cell phone went off. I looked at the screen and saw that the call was from my wife. I flipped it open and said:

"Hello?"

"Rob? I'm at the house and I can't get in. The garage door opener isn't working and none of my keys will fit into the locks."

"Not surprising, Maggie, since you don't live there anymore."

"Of course I live here."

"Where are you, Maggie?"

"I'm at the house."

"I mean, where are you standing right now?"

"On the front porch."

"Look around. You should see a man approaching. His instructions were to wait until he saw you take out your cell phone and make a call before telling you what is going on."

"There is a man coming up the walk right now."

"He will answer all of your questions, Maggie. Goodbye."

Five minutes later, my cell phone chirped again and again it was my wife.

"Rob? What the hell is this nonsense about divorce?"

"No nonsense, Maggie. I just decided that it was time to get rid of a cheating wife."

"Don't be stupid, Rob. I have never cheated on you."

"I'm not being stupid, Maggie. What I am is no longer stupid and blind. Don't bother calling me again. You have been served and the papers have my attorney's name and phone number on them. Any communication between us from now on will have to go through him. And by the way, I moved all of your things out of the house and moved them over to your lover's place. Goodbye, Maggie."

I disconnected, waved over the waitress, and ordered us another round.

***

It started with a phone call from Tom. He asked me to meet him for a drink after work. Tom had been my best friend since the first day of seventh grade. It had been an immediate bond and we had been inseparable all the way through high school. After graduating, I went to college and earned a degree in Business Management and Tom joined the Navy. He served his hitch and when he got out, we reconnected. We saw each once or twice a week, and a month didn't go by that we didn't have a cookout in either his back yard or mine.

I met him at Murphy's Tavern. He was already there seated at a table in the back and I waved at Sally as I walked by the bar and she immediately popped the top on a Coors and handed it to Sherri to bring over to me. I sat down opposite Tom and said:

"What's up?"

"It ain't good bud and I'm not going to come off looking too good here so I need to set the stage. Remember how we were in high school? If a girl didn't put out on the first date, she didn't get a second one and our philosophy was if she did put out on the first date, the first wasn't enough and four was too many?"

"Yeah, but that is ancient history."

"Yes and no. What it did was convince me that sex was entertainment. It was fun. It wasn't something to take seriously. You know and I know you know that Barb and I are swingers. We keep it away from the people we know, unless they approach us on it, and just swing with groups from out of town. Barb thinks just like I do. Sex is fun. Sex is meant to be enjoyed. It has nothing to do with love and devotion. I love Barb to death and everyone knows it and it does not bother me to see her enjoy herself with someone else because I know she will be going home with me and will spend her life trying to spoil me rotten"

"What does that have to do with me?"

"I'm getting to it. When I got out of the Navy, we didn't chase women like we used to. For one thing, I had met Barb and had decided she was the one for me and you were dating Maggie. And then of course there was the fact that we were older and a little more grown up. I married Barb and you married Maggie and the next six years flew happily by until two weeks ago."

"What happened two weeks ago?"

"Two weeks ago you sat here at this very same table and after three or four beers you told me that you felt that there was something wrong in your marriage and then you said, and I quote, 'If I didn't know better I would say Maggie is cheating on me.' Remember that?"

"Yeah, I do."

"Well, Rob that is what brings me here today. Maggie is cheating on you."

"You've got to be kidding?"

"I'm not. Maggie has been cheating on you."

"You are serious?"

"As serious as death."

"How long have you known?"

"That's a hard question to give a straight answer to."

"Damn it, Tom, you brought it up so get to it."

"Okay. I've known for two weeks. She has been cheating on you since before you got married."

"Have you been drinking all day?"

"Of course not. Why the hell would you ask that?"

"Because what you said makes absolutely no sense. You have only known her for two weeks, but you know she was cheating before we got married. We got married over six years ago, Tom."

"I know what she has been doing since before you were married. But I've only known it was cheating since our talk two weeks ago. This is the part where I don't come off looking too good. Given how much we were alike way back, when I just naturally assumed that you were like me; sex was fun, sex was entertainment. Sex wasn't any big deal and it had nothing to do with love, devotion, and stuff like that.

"I knew you weren't like me and Barb, but that didn't mean you didn't have your own ways. Some guys like to watch their wives with other men. Some guys like to send the wife out to play and then listen to her talk about it when she gets home. A lot of guys get a kick out of having a slut for a wife and then there are guys who can't keep up with their wives sexually and to keep the peace in the family they let her go out and play. There are guys who don't care what the wife does as long as she always comes home to them. I assumed that you were one of those kinds of guys."

"Why in the hell would you assume something like that?"

"Why wouldn't I? Maggie has been doing it at least twice a week for over six years, so how could you not know? I mean, come on, Rob. I can see hiding cheating for six or maybe eight months, but six years? I assumed you had to know and just like you knew about Barb and me and never mentioned it, I never mentioned it to you about what I thought you and Maggie had been going. And now comes the 'As well as you know me and you can think that about me,' am I right?"

I looked at him thoughtfully for a few moments and then said, "No, not at all. If it has been going on as long as you say I can see the reasoning behind your thinking. What I can't believe is that it could have been going on as long as it has and I didn't have a clue. It had only been over the last month or so that I began to feel that something wasn't right. So I guess the obvious questions now are who, when, and where."

I listened as Tom told me everything that he knew for sure, everything that he suspected and everything he had heard from others. When he was done, I sat there shaken to my very core.

"What are you going to do?" Tom asked.

"Get some proof and then burn the bitch's ass."

\*\*\*

As I drove home, I thought back to when I'd met Maggie. My brother Jerry and his wife Christina had invited me over for a Sunday afternoon barbecue. No sooner I'd walked in the door when Christina grabbed me by the arm and told me that she had someone she wanted me to meet.

It wasn't the first time Christy had tried playing matchmaker. Whoever the candidate was that day, she would be the seventh since my breakup with Marsha. Marsha had been my long-term girlfriend (three years worth) until the day she told me that she was going out on a date with another guy on Saturday. She picked a really bad time to do it. I had the ring in my pocket and had intended to propose that night. I just looked at her for several very long seconds and then I said:

"I hope you have a nice time." And I took the ring box out of my pocket, opened it, looked at the ring, and then said, "I guess I'll return this tomorrow."

I got up from where I had been sitting and walked away from her as she cried:

"Wait, Rob, wait."

She called me two or three times a day for the next two weeks, but I never took her calls and eventually she stopped calling.

Anyway, there was Christy trying to set me up with another "girl who is just perfect for you." I'd told her more than once not to do it anymore, but she never listened. She didn't understand that I didn't want another girl in my life at that time. I was still hurting from Marsha. I pulled my arm away from Christy's hand and said, "No, Christina, not this time"; and I walked away from her to go find the beer.

There were maybe two-dozen people there and I knew at least half of them. As I made the rounds and socialized, I checked out the women present just to see if I could guess which one Christina wanted to saddle me with. Christina must have thought there was a specific type I would be interested in and all of the previous seven (none of whom I would have gone after if I was looking for Marsha's replacement) were pretty much the same so I was looking for another one like them. I could not see anyone who fit the type.

I did however spot a raven-haired beauty who made my pulse sped up. She was surrounded by guys, one of whom was no doubt the husband, fiancée, or boyfriend. No way in the world that someone hadn't latched onto that. Still, nothing; ventured, nothing gained.

I set my empty beer bottle on a table and walked over to where the gorgeous woman was holding court. I walked up and said to the woman:

"Excuse me for interrupting, but Christina sent me over here to get you."

"And you are?"

"I'm Rob. Christina is my sister-in-law."

"Well, we must not keep her waiting. Lead on."

I noticed that she had been drinking white wine, and I walked her over to the makeshift bar and offered to refill her glass.

"I thought we were going to see, Christina."

"No, what I said was that Christina sent me to get you."

"Are you going to explain that to me?"

"When I got here, Christina told me that there was some one here that she wanted me to meet. Her exact words were: "She is just perfect for you Rob." She was grabbed by someone before she could introduce me to this perfect lady so I walked around looking and there you were."

She gave me an appraising glance and then said, "And you knew right away I was perfect for you?"

"I could see it all the way from the other side of the room."

Just then Christina walked up to us. "Oh good, you found each other. Maggie this is Rob. Rob meet Maggie O'neil."

Maggie and I both broke out laughing and Christy gave us a confused look and said:

"What? What did I say? Why are you laughing?"

Still chuckling, I said, "I forgive you, Christy. I think this time you got it right."

"This time?" Maggie asked.

"A long story, and I'll tell you all about it on our first date which I'm hoping will be tomorrow."

It began, and it was a courtship that ended six months later when Maggie and I exchanged our vows in front of a municipal judge with Christina and my brother Jerry as witnesses.

***

It took every ounce of my self-control to act normally when I got home. Maggie greeted me with a kiss and told me that dinner would be ready in twenty minutes. I grabbed a beer from the fridge and went into the family room, turned on the TV, and tuned it to Fox News. As I listened to the talking heads drone on and on about inconsequential bullshit, I sat there and wondered how Maggie could tell me day after day that she loved me while all the time cheating on me behind my back. Six years! Actually, it was more than six years since she was doing it while we were still dating.

Tuesdays, Thursdays, some Saturdays and always whenever I went out of town on business trips is what Tom had told me. Tuesday was card night with the girls she went to college with, sorority sisters that she stayed in touch with. Thursday was book-club night at the library. That meant that as soon as dinner was over she was going to kiss me, tell me not to wait up, and she would leave to play bridge except that now I knew that thirty minutes after kissing me, she would be lying on a bed with her legs spread for her lovers. Yes, not lover, but lovers.

I got my kiss and as soon as she was gone, I was on the internet. It took me a little less than five minutes to find what I wanted. A credit card number and a couple of key clicks and what I wanted would be delivered to my office within three working days. I looked at my watch and saw that I still had time to get to Radio Shack before it closed. By the time Maggie got home from "bridge," the house phone had a tap on it and I was in bed pretending to be asleep.

Even though before we had often made love when Maggie came home from her card nights, on those occasions I had never known I was the second or third that night. While I would have sex with Maggie on some nights—not to do so would raise a red flag—I would never again let myself follow someone else.

In the mornings, I usually left for work before Maggie and I almost always got home after she did so I had no chance to check on the phone tap until Thursday evening when Maggie left the house for her so-called book club meeting. Wednesday morning, Maggie had called her mother and had talked for about five minutes and then:

"Hi. You okay?"

"I'm fine."

"You didn't seem like your usual self last night."

"I guess I'm just a little worried."

"About what?"

"Rob. He's acting a little funny."

"You think he knows or suspects something?"

"I don't know. It is just a feeling I have. I don't have anything concrete, just a feeling."

"You want to cancel tomorrow night?"

"No, because if he is suspicious I'm afraid it would make him curious as to why all of a sudden after years of going, I suddenly stopped. I guess we have to keep it like business as usual. Both of you need to stay on your toes and make sure that you don't do anything that will give us away."

"I'll tell him. We don't want it to get out either."

There was only one call on Thursday. "Hi."

"Hi yourself. We still on for tonight?"

"Wouldn't miss it."

"Love you."

"Love you too, baby, see you in an hour."

Once again I was faking being asleep when Maggie came home, and it took all I had in me not to flinch when she cuddled up next to me on the bed.

* * *

Friday, my package arrived. I opened it and familiarized myself with the directions. It was a wireless mini-camera disguised as a book. It was motion activated and sent its signal to a receiver that could be up to three-hundred feet away. According to Tom, my wife and her lovers sometimes used our house when I was away on business. I suspect that it was so that Maggie could be home if I called. My plan was to set the book in place the next time I went out of town and hope that Maggie did her thing at our place.

As I was putting the unit into the trunk of my car, I was thinking about Tuesday's phone call. I needed to get my head out of my ass and make damned sure that Maggie got over that "feeling" she was having, and there was only one way to do it. When I got home, Maggie was in the kitchen fixing dinner. I walked up behind her, reached around her, and cupped her tits in my hands and said:

"Turn off the stove. I'm having desert first tonight."

"Is this desert going to be cream filled?"

"I wouldn't be at all surprised."

She twisted the knobs to the two lit burners to the off position, and I picked her up and carried her to the bedroom. I made it a point to do it again Saturday morning and Sunday night and hopefully that took care of uneasiness.

***

Monday, I told Maggie that I would be going to San Diego for four days the following week. Tuesday, I even bit the bullet and waited up for her and we had sex (no love making, just sex) before falling asleep. Her telephone conversations never again contained mentions that Maggie thought I was behaving strangely.

Friday, I listened to the tape from the tap and heard that Maggie would be visiting her lovers before going to her standing appointment with her hairdresser and I heard what I'd hoped to hear.

"I suppose we will be doing it at your place next week while he is gone?"

"Of course. You know I have to be here when Rob makes his nightly check-in call."

"I can't wait for next week. No hurrying, no rushing to get you home. I love it when we can spend the whole night together."

"I do too, baby."

"I have to be going. I need to get hubby's dinner on the stove."

We had sex Friday night, Sunday afternoon, and the then on Monday morning, I left on my trip. As I kissed Maggie goodbye, I was aware of the fact that if the book camera worked as advertised and caught what I expected it to catch Maggie, I would no longer be living together with her a week from then.

***

The camera did do its job, but it didn't catch both of Maggie's lovers. It confused me at first since I had expected to have footage of both of them, but then I shrugged it off since I had more than enough for my purpose.

I tried to act normally around Maggie over the weekend. I met Tom for a beer on Saturday and we made our plans for Monday. At ten o'clock, well after Maggie had left for work, Tom, Phil, Mike and I met at my house and moved everything of Maggie's out. At eleven, the locksmith was there and all the locks were changed and the garage door opener was reprogrammed. The previous week, I had seen an attorney and got the paperwork started on the divorce, but we held off on serving the papers until I had the visual proof that I wanted. Monday morning, I called him and told him to have them served.

***

Phil and Mike had already gone so it was just Tom and I sitting at Murphy's when Tom said:

"Ready or not, it's show time."

My brother Jerry stormed up to where we were sitting. He was boiling mad and he said:

"You bastard! What do you mean by suing Christina and me for alienation of affection? Are you fucking crazy?"

"No, but you must have been, to think you could get away with it forever."

"You are out of your mind if yo…"

"Get the fuck out of here, Jerry, while you can still do it under your own power."

"Don't threaten me, you little asshole." Jerry was six three and I was only five eleven so I was little to him.

I stood up and hit him. I caught him right on the chin and he went glassy eyed and started to stagger and I hit him twice more and he fell to the floor. I'd already warned Gus behind the bar what was likely to happen and he just kept drying glasses. I looked down at Jerry and then I kicked him in the crotch and was drawing back to kick him again when Tom pulled me back.

"Enough, bud. I think he has a pretty good idea of how you feel. I don't know if he has the balls to charge you with assault, but let's not make it any worse than it is."

Jerry was struggling to get up when I said, "Mom and dad are going to be so proud of you."

"You wouldn't dare."

"I'm having dinner with them Wednesday night and they are bound to ask me why Maggie isn't there with me. Want to guess what I'm going to tell them? Oh, by the way, I took the key you gave me when you asked me to watch your place when you were on vacation and used it to get into your house and move all of Maggie's shit into your spare bedroom. She can stay there all the time now instead of just Tuesdays and Thursdays."

I turned to Tom and said, "Let's get the hell out of here." I waved at Gus and he waved back and we left.

\*\*\*

Maggie's car was parked in the drive when I got home, and she was sitting in it waiting for me. I hit the button on the garage door opener, edged around Maggie, pulled into the garage, and hit the button to close the door. Maggie got out of her car and ran to try and get in the garage before the door closed, but didn't make it. I went on into the house, hoping that she would go away but knowing that she wouldn't.

The front door bell started ringing and I knew it would keep ringing until I went to the door so I decided to just get it over with. I had foreseen the eventuality, and after the locksmith was done, I locked the screen doors on the front and back doors and the patio. I opened the door and Maggie tried to pull the screen door open, but it wouldn't budge.

"Let me in, Rob."

"Nothing in here for you, Maggie. All of your stuff has been moved over to Jerry and Christina's place. You live in their spare bedroom now. It will save on the travel time you used to have to spend on Tuesdays and Thursdays."

"We need to talk, Rob."

"No, we don't. The time for the talk should have been the day I asked you to marry me. What should have happened on that day is that you should have said:

"Oh gee, Rob, I don't know. I have long term lovers that I don't want to give up. If you can see your way clear to share me with them of course I will marry you."

"I would have said sorry, no thanks, and we could have been spared for what we are going through right now."

"I need to explain, Rob."

"Probably," I said as I cut her off, "but while you feel the need to explain I don't feel the need to listen. All talking is through my attorney from now on," and I closed the door in her face.

Maggie beat on the door for another fifteen or twenty minutes, but I just turned the volume up on the TV and ignored her.

***

The next day started out badly, and then it got worse. I was making my morning coffee when the phone rang. It was Jerry.

"We need to talk, Rob. You've got the wrong idea. Things are not what you think they are and you need to let me explain."

"Maggie used the same words last night, and I'll tell you just what I told her. You may feel the need to explain, but I have no need or desire to hear it. Stay out of my life, Jerry. Don't call, don't come to see me, and don't send me emails or snail mail. As far as I'm concerned, you are dead to me and I don't ever want to see you or hear your voice again."

I hung up on him and then began building myself a breakfast. I was still simmering from the call from Jerry when the phone rang again. It was my mother.

"Don't forget that you are coming over for dinner tomorrow night. Your Aunt Grace is going to be in town tomorrow, and I'm having the whole family over for dinner."

"Will Jerry and Christina be there?"

"Of course."

"Then I'll have to pass."

"Why on earth would you say that?"

"Jerry and Christina are no longer in my life, and if you want to know why, ask them about their six-year sexual affair."

"Oh my God, Rob, you can't mean that."

"Unfortunately, I do."

"Six years? But you have only been married for six years."

"Apparently, it was going on even before Maggie and I got married."

"Oh, baby, I'm so sorry."

"Give my love to Aunt Grace and make up some excuse as to why I can't be there. I'll talk to you later."

I hated like hell, putting my mom in the position of having to juggle family events to allow for the fact that I would not ever be where Jerry was, but I would have had to tell her eventually why I never showed up for dinners and the like so sooner rather than later was my decision. That and the fact that the sooner she knew the sooner she could go after Jerry.

After disconnecting from mom, I started going through the house making a list of what I needed to do to make the house more marketable. I was under no illusion about keeping the house. For one thing, we lived in a state where no-fault divorce was the norm so the house would need to be sold because we would have to split the proceeds. Another, the house was way too big for one person. We had bought the big four bedroom with a future family in mind. The plan had been to start having children when we reached thirty. Until thirty, we wanted to be free to go places and do things that we knew wouldn't be possible when children came along. Now I was glad we had waited. Putting kids through a divorce is never a good thing.

I was on the patio looking at what needed to be done in the back yard when a voice behind me said, "Afternoon, Rob."

I turned and saw Christina standing there.

"What do you want?"

"To talk. You won't talk to Maggie or Jerry so I thought I'd try. At least, I don't think you'll hit me like you did Jerry."

"No need to talk, Christina. You don't have anything that I either want or need to hear."

"Since when have I been, Christina? It has always been Chrissy or Chris."

"That was before I found out about you stabbing me in the back for the last six years."

"It isn't wha…"

"Don't try to bullshit me, Christina. I wired the house before my last out-of-town trip. I have it all on DVD, Christina, so save your lies. Now, please leave. I won't hit you like I hit Jerry, but if you don't leave on your own I'll pick you up and carry you off my property."

"You do that and I'll file assault charges against you. You can call the cops and have them evict me from your property, but if you touch me without my permission I'll burn you."

I locked eyes with her and held my gaze on her as I took out my cell phone. "So be it," I said as I started pushing buttons on the phone.

"What are you doing?"

"Taking your advice and calling the cops."

"Damn it, Rob, why won't you be reasonable and hear me out?"

"Because I don't want to."

"All right, all right, I'll go." And she turned and walked around the side of the house and out the gate. I disconnected the call and went back to scoping out the yard.

\*\*\*

I spent the next two days refusing to take Maggie's phone calls at work, on the home phone, or my cell. My evenings at home were spent on the projects I had listed as being needed to get the house in saleable shape. I was in the bathroom downstairs working on a leaking shower door when I heard a loud noise from the kitchen. I went there and got there in time to see Maggie climbing in through a broken window.

"What the hell are you doing here?"

"Getting into my house. Since my key won't work anymore, this is the way I've chosen to do it."

"You aren't supposed to be here."

"This is my house just as much as it is yours and just because you say I don't live here anymore, doesn't make it so. You really should have looked for a better lawyer, Rob. Your divorce paperwork doesn't say anything about who gets the primary residence pending the decision of the court. That has been corrected by the way. I saw an attorney and he told me that absent such wording in your divorce petition, I have as much right to be here as you do. My petition has the proper wording in it so after you are served you will have to move out."

"Your petition?"

"I'm countersuing."

"On what grounds?"

"We are no fault, Rob, so I don't need grounds but my attorney said it would be wise to put in a reason so I'm claiming extreme mental cruelty."

"How are you going to prove that?"

"I don't need to prove it, Rob. That's what no fault means. I simply say that I want out because of mental cruelty and if there are no extenuating circumstances, the paperwork is rubber and it is done."

"But it isn't true."

"So?"

"So it becomes public record and if anyone for any reason does a records search, I'll come out looking less than good."

"So?"

"Okay, if that's the way you want to play it, I'll talk to my lawyer tomorrow and have him change my petition from irreconcilable differences to adultery and we will see how you come out looking if your name turns up in a records search and just to make it interesting I have proof of my claim and you don't."

"You don't have any proof."

"Oh but I do. A little birdie told me that you were cheating on me so I wired the house before I went on my last business trip. I have you on a DVD in living color cheating on me in our bedroom and on our bed."

"Is that what this is all about? Me and Chrissy?"

"And Jerry."

"Jerry? What has Jerry got to do with it?"

"Don't play dumb, Margaret Estelle. You know damned well what Jerry has to do with it. The three of you stabbing me in the back since before we were even married."

I saw something come over her face, like someone had suddenly turned on a light bulb.

"Oh no, oh no, Rob, you have it all wrong. There is absolutely nothing going on between me and Jerry. There has never been anything between me and Jerry. Between me and Chris, yes, but never Jerry."

"That's not the story I got. You visit Jerry and Christina every Tuesday and Thursday when you are supposed to be playing cards and going to book club meetings."

"Sometimes Jerry is home and sometimes he isn't. Even when he is home, he stays in his den or works in the basement. Jerry has never been part of what Chris and I do. He knows about it of course, but he also knows that Christy loves him and is never going to go looking for another man and knowing that he lets her have her little pleasures."

"So you admit to cheating on me."

"Of course not. Cheating implies that I'm taking something away from you and giving it to someone else."

"And that is just what you were doing."

"No, I was not. Did I ever say no to you when you wanted to make love except for when I had my monthly? No, I didn't, and even then I always gave you head if you wanted it. And who was the instigator half of the time we made love? I was. Has our sex life suffered because of my time with Chris? No, it hasn't. We are still making love four and five times a week. Ask our married friends how they are doing and I'll bet you that the average is twice a week. Can you point to any one thing over the past six years that would show that I didn't love you or care for you?"

I was silent. On that, so she went on.

"No you cannot. Do we snuggle or cuddle any less? You cannot point to anything that says I don't love you or that I am depriving you of anything. My thing with Chris has not cost you a thing."

"Your thing with Christina?"

"I am bi-sexual, Rob, and I have been since summer camp when I fell in with two girls who were also bi. Chris was my roommate all through college and we recognized the signs in each other immediately. We were lovers all through college and after. It has been almost eleven years now that we have been taking care of each other's bi-sexual urges."

"It is still cheating, and you know it. The fact that you have lied to me for six years about what you do on Tuesdays and Thursdays, some Saturdays and whenever I'm gone proves that you know what you are doing is wrong."

"No, it does not. All it proves is that I love too much to let you know because I knew how you would take it and you knowing would most likely would have split us apart."

"Of course knowing that you were cheating would split us apart."

"Damn it, Rob, I was not cheating. I didn't tell you what I was doing because of what is going on in your head right now. You are a homophobe, Rob, and you know it. I can't even begin to count the number of derogatory remarks you have directed at people who are not heterosexual. If I would have told you I was bi-sexual, you would have taken it to mean I was queer, a dyke, or whatever else you use as a disparaging remark for people who don't think about sex as you do so I never let you know. I need what I get from Chris that I can't get from you."

"So you are saying that I don't satisfy you in the bedroom."

"No, damn it. That is not what I am saying. I am extremely satisfied with you in bed, but you don't have a pussy I can eat. You do not have breasts that I can play with and suck. You are not a woman, Rob, and I occasionally need a woman. I need you and I need what I get from Chris. Bi means both, Rob. I need a man and that is you and I need a woman and that is Christina. I need you both."

There was silence for several seconds and then Maggie said, "What now, Rob? Do we call the lawyers and tell them to tear up the paperwork. Do we put this behind us and get on with our marriage?"

"I don't know that it would be possible, Maggie. You have destroyed my trust. Do I know that Christina is the only one you have cheated on me with? Do I know that there isn't a man you see occasionally? Do I know that you really had nothing to do with Jerry? I only have your word that Christina is the only one, but what is your word worth? You are too good at lying, Maggie. You have lied to me for six years without me ever having a clue. But even if you aren't lying, you were still cheating.

"Paint it anyway you want to, Maggie, but to me it is still cheating. A sexual relationship of any kind with someone other than your spouse is cheating. Can I get over it? Maybe if I work at it, but can you? Can you with your bi nature get used to only having one half of what you say you need. Can you give up Christina and be happy with only me?"

"I'm not giving up Christina, Rob."

"Then you have just answered your own question."

"What? What question."

"You asked if we should call the lawyers and tell them to tear up the paperwork and you just answered the question. The answer is no, we don't call them."

"I didn't say that."

"Yes, you did. When I asked if you could give up Christina and be happy with just me you chose Christina."

"Oh come on, Rob, be reasonable. I explained it all to you."

"You explained from your standpoint and as far as you are concerned it is not a problem, but from my standpoint it is a problem. I will not share my spouse with anyone—man or woman—and if my spouse has sexual relations with anyone other than me, she is cheating and I will not tolerate it."

"You are serious? You are going to throw away what we've had over this? Okay, Rob, I will give up Chris. Are you happy now?"

"No, Maggie, it is too late for that now."

"Why? I'm giving you what you want."

"Yes, and you are doing it reluctantly. You don't want to and as far as you are concerned, I am forcing you to do it. You resent it and over time that resentment will build and affect our relationship even more. You still don't believe that you have done anything wrong, and if the opportunity ever presents itself that lets you think you can do it and get away with it, you will. Our only chance was when I asked if you could be happy with only me; you replied yes, that you couldn't go on without me, or couldn't live without me or something along those lines. What I got was an emphatic, "I'm not giving up Christina, Rob"; and that put the final nail in the coffin.

"No, Maggie, the only way our marriage could have continued would have been for me to never find out. Unfortunately for us, I did. Go enjoy Christina and look for a man who can accept it. Just make sure you let him know before you marry him."

*** 

Maggie never did countersue and the divorce went through. It hurt because I did love Maggie and I probably always will, but it just isn't in my makeup to condone cheating even when she didn't believe she was. I guess there is a price to be paid for having and holding to old-fashioned values.

Maggie did remarry, but whether she told him of her proclivities before they took their vows, I have no way of knowing. I do know that she lived in Jerry and Christina's spare bedroom until she remarried.

The breech between my brother and me never healed. The fact that Maggie said he never touched her meant nothing to me because he had known what she was doing and that she was hiding it from me and he covered for her and as far as I was concerned, that was just as bad. I was able to reach a point where I could attend family gatherings if he and Christina were there, but I kept my distance from them and we never spoke to each other although Christina kept trying.

I finally met a girl I liked enough to date more than once and after six months, she started indicating that she wanted to make things permanent. I asked her if she had any secrets that it would be best for me to learn before we got married and she asked, "What kind of secrets?" I told her about my marriage to Maggie and she laughed as she said:

"I've munched a carpet or two in my time, but I'm not all that into them. I much prefer cocks and I am a firm believer in fidelity."

I married Betty and we are getting along just fine. In fact, she is expecting and I'm going to be a daddy in six months.

# The End

*Watch out for *Erotica Short Stories, Vol. 11 – 9 Shades Of Sex*

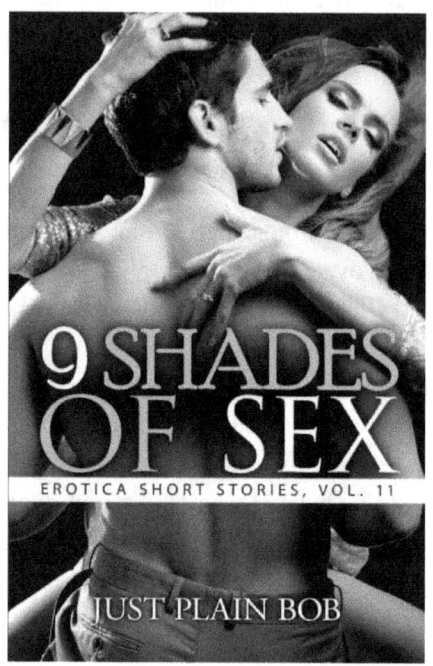

**Also by this Author:**

**From the Author**

If you enjoyed any of my books then please share the love and promote my books in Amazon.

If you write me a review and send me an email I will send you a free book, or many.
(Just know that these emails are filtered by my publisher.)

Good news is always welcome.

One Last Thing, For Kindle Readers...

When you turn the page, Kindle will give you the opportunity to rate this book and share your thoughts on Facebook and Twitter. If you enjoyed my writings, would you please take a few seconds to let your friends know about it? Because... when they enjoy they will be grateful to you and so will I.

Thank You!

# An Open Letter from Just Plain Bob

*A message for those who like my stories, those who hate my stories, those who are indifferent and those who have yet to make up their minds.*

I have often stated that I really don't care what others think about my stories, that I write for my own enjoyment and then I offer to share. If you like my stories fine and if you don't, also fine since I have already satisfied my target audience - me!

It is human nature to strive to get better. If you take up bowling your first games are going low scoring, but you will work and practice to get better and as your average climbs you may forget the game where you had three gutter balls and shot an eighty-six, but that game is still there in your past.

Your first time on the golf course you shot an eighty on the front nine, but did you settle for that being your game or did you work to improve? You may eventually get a three handicap, but that nine hole eighty is still there as part of your past.

When you hired in at your job did you say, "Cool, I got it made" and do nothing more than what you barely had to do or did you go to work thinking that, "Someday I'm going to be running this place." You might never climb that high, but human nature says that you are going to at least try.

It is the same with authors who write stories and post them on sites like Literotica. Their first stories might not be all that good, but comments and feedback along with a desire to get better drive them toward putting out a better product or to at least try.

I'm no different. My first stories might not have been all that great, but they are still there on the hard drive. I like cheating wife stories and five years ago I found my first adult site that catered to cheating wife stories. It was a pay site, but it had a policy of giving a free lifetime membership to anyone who submitted five stories to the site. How hard can that be I said to myself as I sat down and fired up the word processor and went to work.

I sent my five stories in and sat back to enjoy my free membership and a funny thing happened. I started getting feedback, most of it positive, and I became hooked. I started cranking out more stories. The site I was sending my stories to had seven categories:

*Bisexual*
*Cream Pie*

*Groups*
*I Watch*
*Gang Bang*
*Racial*
*SM/BD*

I know nothing about bisexual or SM/BD and I had no interest in Groups so all the stories I wrote I tailored for the four remaining categories:

*Cream Pie*
*I Watch*
*Gang Bang*
*Racial.*

I turned out eight stories a month, two for each category, which means that after five years I have over 120 stories in each of those categories and they are all still on the hard drive.

A year ago I received an email asking me why I never posted stories on Literotica. The answer? I didn't know about Lit. I pulled it up, liked what I saw, and started sending in stories to it. All new stories? No, not hardly, not with over 400 stories sitting on the hard drive. Maybe one new story for each fifteen or so old ones. The newer ones are better, at least I think they are and I have received some feedback that leads me to believe that others think so too, and I will continue to write new ones.

But I am still going to recycle what is on the hard drive, stories that were written specifically to fit the four categories. That means that those of you who hate cream pie stories still have eighty or so to look forward to. Ditto for those who call me a racist; you will get another seventy or so interracial stories.

Those who hate wimps will only see about fifty more of those because the stories I sent to the I Watch category were split 50/50 between what some call wimps and some call "real men." Why the 50/50 split? It came from listening to the readers. I would get feedback asking me why all the men in my stories were hard asses. "In real life men are more forgiving, especially if it is the first indiscretion." So I would write stories with forgiving husbands and boyfriends and then the next batch of feedback would say, "Why are all your husbands spineless wimps" and I'd write stories that went back the other way.

Eventually I came to realize that I was wasting my time - there was no way I could write a story that would satisfy everybody and that is when I adopted my philosophy of writing for my own enjoyment and then offering to share.

As far as the gangbang stories? Well, what can I say? Gangbangs are gangbangs and there are still eighty or so of them to go.

The bottom line is that Literotica readers are going to see more of my old stories than my new ones. If I'm still around three or four years from now it will probably go the other way, more new than old.

I feel the need to respond to some of the comments and emails I have received. By far the largest percentage comes from people who say, "You are an asshole because all women are not whores and sluts and that's all you make them out to be."

Next most common is, "You must really hate women you sick fuck."

"You must be a wimp because all the men in your stories are wimps" is up there in the top ten along with, "Why don't you give it a rest and go crawl off in a hole somewhere."

There is a lot more, but I'm only going to address those four and in reverse order.

I won't stop and go crawl in a hole because I am enjoying the hell out of what I am doing and remember what I said, I am doing this for MY OWN ENJOYMENT and then I offer to share. Some obviously like my sharing with them and so I will continue to do so. No one is holding a gun to a reader's head and telling them they must click on a Just Plain Bob story or die. It is a conscious choice on the reader's part to move that mouse and click on that story.

When a man finds out he has a cheating wife or girlfriend there are only a limited number of ways he can handle it. If he loves her he can forgive, try to forget and try to hold on and somehow make things work. He can turn his back on her, walk away and get on with his life. The third option is to take revenge.

According to a good portion of those who send me feedback the first and second options are proof that the men are wimps. If the man takes the third option he is still considered a wimp if he doesn't do some sort of physical damage to the woman and her lover. These readers believe that the only way not to be a wimp is to kill, maim and destroy everything in sight. Doing that however, will invariably get the man throw in jail and that is why it so rarely happens in real life.

In real life most revenge takes place in the man's head when he says to himself, "I should have _____ (fill in the blank) the fucking cunt!" I know this because I have been there and done that (see The Dark Trilogy). In my stories I try to mirror real life so kill, maim and destroy are going to be for the most part absent. Outside of some fisticuffs there will be very little physical violence in my stories. Most of my husbands are going to do what I did, what several of my friends and others that I know have done, forgive, or walk away. If this makes them wimps and me a wimp for writing the story that way, so be it.

Next is the "I must hate all women." Nothing could be farther from the truth. I love women. I lust after women. I even like whores and sluts. I have been married four times, engaged two other times (that did not end in marriage) and I have always had girlfriends between marriages. My philosophy is that women were put on this earth for me to enjoy and I'm not talking just sexually. I could sit at the mall (and have) for hours and just girl watch.

The engagements, girlfriends and three of the four marriages bring me to the #1 anti JPB comment on the list.

"You are an asshole because all women aren't whores and sluts."

Well dear reader, you can not prove that by me! I will say up front that I KNOW all women aren't whores and sluts, BUT the majority of the women in my life were. My mother ran around on my father for years while he was driving a truck for a living. My Aunt Margaret cheated regularly on my Uncle Bill, as did my Aunt Mildred on my Uncle Paul. My Aunt Betty fucked around on my Uncle Bob for years and finally left him for his brother, my Uncle Wendell. Uncle Wendell in turn caught her on her knees at his company Christmas party giving Season's Greetings to his boss.

My sister is three times divorced and each divorce came about when the then current husband caught her out spreading pollen. Both of the engagements I mentioned ended when I found out that I was not the one and only and a lot of the girls I dated between marriages never made it to engagement status for the same reason.

And that brings me to my three ex-wives. The first one, Helen (I believe I commented on her in the intro to The Dark Trilogy) had seven different lovers before I found out what was going on. I was living proof that love is blind. Ditto with my second wife. She had a secret life that she hid from me and when I found out about her brother, his friends and the gangbangs she was history.

My third marriage ended in divorce because of a different kind of cheating (and I can just imagine the outrage I am going to get over this) - she cheated on me with an idea. I was away from home on business, she was lonely, a couple of Jehovah's Witnesses knocked on the door and my wife, with nothing better to do invited them in. When I came home from my trip I found out that she had found God. On a scale that runs from TRUE BELIEVER on one end to ATHEIST on the other you will find me just to the right of AGNOSTIC and since I would not allow myself to be SAVED the marriage eventually died.

So yes, I write about sluts and whores because as everyone knows, you tend to write about the things you know. And I do like sluts and whores, just not the ones that lie to me and cheat on me.

So be forewarned - if you click on a Just Plain Bob story you will be getting sluts, whores and husbands who do not kill, maim and destroy. There are other things you will rarely find in a Just Plain Bob story. Even though I try to mirror real life my stories all take place in StoryLand. In StoryLand STDs and un-wanted pregnancies do not exist unless the author feels like they may add something to the story. Bad things do not happen in StoryLand unless the author so wills it and no amount of "You should have…" in comments and feedback will change a story already posted.

Lastly, I will touch on a truth. None of what I have written here means shit because the same readers will still read the same stories that they profess to hate and make the same comments they have always made. Knowing this, I will deliberately post stories that will have them frothing at the mouth.

It is the least I can do for an adoring public.

Thank you!

**Just Plain Bob**
justplainbob@awesomeauthors.org